GENRE PURGE 3

Michael Andre-Driussi

Sirius Fiction

ISBN-13: 978-1-947614-15-4 (paperback)
ISBN-13: 978-1-947614-16-1 (ebook)

Cover illustration by: Donald Iain Smith

CONTENTS

MIRACLE OF ASTEROID CAMP 88

Toothless Tom stuck his head into the gambling den just long enough to say, "Necky's in trouble."

For Shoe the Gambler, who had been placidly studying his bad hand of cards, this distraction seemed as good an excuse as any.

"Well, gentlemen, shall we quit?"

The other men were already heading for the door.

Shoe unbuckled his seatbelt and followed them through the microgravity into Jin's Hydroponics. The store was empty of the usual cracker-barrel crowd, and Jin himself was absent.

Camp 88 was located on an unpromising asteroid, being neither a metallic one, nor an icy one, but a stony one in which metals and ices existed only in traces. When Shoe stepped out of Jin's he was in the downtown area of the main cavern, his mag-slippers keeping his feet against the metal sidewalk.

Necky's place was a battered little pressure shelter anchored on the other side of the road, next to the junk department. A crowd of men was huddled around this hut, a crowd which grew as he watched. He whistled softly in surprise when he saw miners that had come straight from their diggings. *Must be the entire population now,* he thought.

"Oh, so that's it," said an out of breath voice that came up beside him. Shoe turned to see Supervisor Young, a big fat man who was the nearest thing to a mayor that the settlement had. "I thought it was a fight," he said, looking relieved.

"Not likely to draw a crowd, these days," said Shoe.

"Yeah," said Toothless Tom, floating over to join them. "The last fight was way back when Beijing Beau and Slippery Mike shot each other in Jin's front room. You fellers in the poker room didn't even take a peek." He reached down toward Shoe for an assist.

"I had a winning hand," said Shoe. He drew Tom down so his feet stuck to the walk.

"Anybody in there now?" asked Young, wiping his sopping forehead with a greasy sleeve. More men were drifting over into his orbit, like captured moons circling a gas giant.

"Nah, they all came out," said Shoe. "And you're the last to arrive, so now everybody's here."

Young took a breath and blew it out.

"Well," he said, "this has been brewing for half

a year, at least."

"Nine months," said Shoe.

"She just started, like, an hour ago?" asked Young.

"Turns out she started a couple days ago," said Tom.

"That's a bad sign," said Young, hands on his hips.

Loitering there at the periphery, they spoke in low tones about Necky the catgirl.

"How'd she get here in the first place?" said Young.

"Damned if I know," said Tom, "but oh, seems like she's been around forever. Nearly a year, don't you think?"

"That's right," said Young. "Right near the beginning, she was here."

"Perhaps," said Shoe, "she came along with that playboy back then, remember him?"

"That perfume-y guy?" said Tom. He sucked his gums and said, "Could be, could be."

"And then she stayed on," said Young.

"Abandoned," said Tom, "or maybe she jumped ship."

"Things went bad," said Shoe. "The last human whores left, the population fell to 100 . . ."

"Ninty-seven," said Young.

". . . but she's still here."

It was ironic that Necky, who had given female companionship to all of the men, was now in dire need of a different sort of female companionship

—someone to tend to her labor pains.

Talk about a bad hand, thought Shoe. *And look at us, all standing around, helpless in the face of it. Hell, somebody's going to do something, and it isn't going to be me.* And that's when he came up with a plan.

"That's rough, the spot she's in," he said to Young.

"Yes, it is," said Young, bobbing his head like a judge. "It is, indeed."

"If I remember right," said Shoe, scratching at his cheek, "you've had experience with wives and kids."

"Sure, that's why I—hey, just a second! What are you saying?"

"I'm just saying that, among all of us here, you're in the best position to be of some assistance to the lady in distress."

Young felt stirred to action. Casting his eyes about in near panic, he caught sight of Doc lounging in quiet over to the side. With a sudden move Young cornered Doc, a big mass confronting a nimble one.

"You go in there," said Young. "You gotta see what you can do."

"Me?" said Doc. He was deceptively small, wiry in build and very fierce when riled up. "No way. I don't know the first thing."

"You're the best we got, Doc."

"We all know I'm just a medic," said Doc, looking around for support while tugging on his beard in agitation.

They pushed him in.

Necky's pregnancy was something so unusual as to be almost a miracle. The men debated how it was even possible, given that she was a b-bot, a biological construct of human and feline genes.

"I wonder if she'll drop a whole litter," said one, which got a few laughs.

"Now look here," said another. "I growed up on a dirt farm, see? An' I knows how a horse mated with a donkey makes a mule, a what'cha-call 'high-bread,' with the best of both horse and donkey, but excepting it can't breed at all."

Others nodded, since Necky was a hybrid herself. Everybody had figured she was sterile, one way or the other.

Time stretched on and the men began to joke away the tension. Some made bets on Necky surviving, on the baby surviving, and other details—Shoe refused to take part. Tom and Young got to talking about the way gravity assists a woman's labor on Earth and how poor Necky had none of Mother Earth's help. This led to an excited discussion of engineering a solution to the problem, in the middle of which came a yell from those nearest the door, and the population stopped to listen. Above the whirr of the ventilation, the gurgle of the plumbing, and the hum of the light tubes, sounded a sharp, angry cry—a tiny yell unlike anything heard before in that place.

The silence lasted for one breathless moment and then the men roared back, their tension released.

Someone shouted from the front hatch, "It's a boy!" And they roared again.

Doc showed up at the hatch, looking haggard. The excited men around him talked about a cae-sarean section performed with a jack knife. He brushed off their congratulations and demanded that more supplies be brought at once—the new mother was in critical condition.

For the next hour Doc did everything he could. She slipped away despite his efforts.

"Can the boy live?" asked Young.

"Sure, why not?" said Doc. "Mother's milk is just chemicals. Get somebody to look up a for-mula, and whip up a batch at the main kitchen."

"Go on, Shoe," said Young.

"I'm on it," the gambler called over his shoul-der. Things had worked out well, and now that the main thing was done he was glad to put in some work behind the scenes.

First he went over to the main kitchen to see what they had in the way of basic foodstuffs. He was hoping to ask a few questions, but naturally there was nobody there.

Then he hit upon the idea of going online, so he went to the communication section and helped himself to some free computer access. The time lag to Mars was a torturous few minutes each way, but after a lot of typing and pacing around, he got a recipe he could use.

Back at the kitchen he mixed up the first

batch, using powdered milk, water, and a bit of corn syrup. Shoe poured this into an unused vinyl glove and tied the end shut.

Returning to Necky's cabin, he found a line of men waiting to view the baby. Young, stationed at the hatch, waved him over to the head of the line.

He went in. The upper bunk was piled with clothes and feminine knickknacks cleared out from the airlock, which Necky had been using as a closet. On the lower bunk lay Necky's body, shrouded in blankets and lashed down with bungee cords. Beside this squatted a small table magnetically stuck to the floor, with a box velcroed to the top. Inside the box lay the latest arrival, bundled in a pillowcase and lashed with bungee. An upturned space helmet was duct-taped next to this makeshift cradle.

Doc spoke, his voice worn with fatigue and repetition. "Come in, go around the table, and out the back airlock. If you'd like to contribute anything toward the orphan, put it in the helmet."

There were two miners in front of Shoe, who, having no mag-slippers, hovered in the cramped quarters like benign spirits or sooty angels.

"Is that him?" said the one.

"He's tiny," said the other.

"Looks human."

When his turn came, Shoe the Gambler handed the improvised bottle to Doc, then looked at the napping baby. Something stirred in his chest so that he felt like coughing, but he held back to keep from waking the baby.

He glanced into the helmet, his practiced eye calculating the amount it contained in an instant. It was a good sum, not to be dismissed, but he found he wanted to give something more personal. From his pocket he dug out his lucky gold sample and put that into the helmet. Next he added his vial of cologne, won back in the heyday and saved for special occasions. That still wasn't enough, so he put in his best pistol, a fancy derringer. Then he nodded with satisfaction and moved on to let the next man in.

This calls for a drink, thought Shoe, turning his steps toward Jin's.

The place was packed. Shoe got a shot of the good stuff and saluted the baby's safe arrival. Looking around, he couldn't remember the last time he'd seen such excitement at the camp.

After a while, Supervisor Young came in, puffed up and beaming with pride.

"The li'l wizard shook my finger," he said. Everybody raised a toast to that.

The next light period they gave Necky her funeral, after which there was a formal meeting of the camp to discuss the fate of her orphan. A proposal to adopt the infant as a group was met with enthusiasm by nearly all, but the details on how to proceed led to animated discussions. A notion was floated that the child should be sent over to Ceres, the nearest big asteroid, where he could be tended by women. Shoe the Gambler was in favor of this, but to his surprise it met fierce and nearly unanimous opposition. It was plain that they wouldn't let the boy go.

The suggestion of inviting a female nurse to the camp also met with objection. Opponents argued that by definition no decent woman could make the place her home, and one man went so far as to say, "We don't want no more of that other kind." This slur against the newly dead mother, while harsh, was the first spasm of propriety in the history of the settlement.

Doc himself said nothing. After it became clear that nobody else was volunteering, Shoe asked Doc if he might be willing to continue.

"Well," said Doc, his face taking on a kind of glow, "as long as the kitchen can produce formula, and as long as the diaper department can do their job, both coming and going, I can manage to rear the child."

This was something independent and near-heroic, so that it stirred the men with powerful emotions, not the least of which was relief. More men volunteered for the ad hoc diaper department, and in order to get "baby stuff," finances were advanced for a trip to asteroid Juno.

Each of the 96 men living there felt like a father to the boy, to a greater or lesser degree. They had him, and he had all of them.

Change came by tiny steps, radiating outward from the pressure cabin. The men repaired the metal hut and restocked it with emergency supplies that had gone missing long before. Doc kept the place scrupulously clean, having become a fanatic about hygiene. Everybody started cleaning up "for the baby"—dapper Shoe the Gambler passed this requirement, but Supervisor Young was barred from visiting for a while until he improved himself in this regard. And yet, he adjusted, too. Soon he was showing up every day with a washed face and a clean shirt.

The men's rowdy behavior was toned down since the baby needed to sleep. Their rough language was also gradually cleaned up. By these voluntary stages, civilization came to the frontier.

Weeks passed and the child thrived. Shoe got a peaceful feeling whenever Doc brought the baby over to Jin's place, where he would set the infant among the grow lamps and the green leaves of the hydroponics rooms. The men talked about Vitamin D and took a new interest in plants. Jin expanded the hydroponics section with the hope of adding a few ornamental plants, a few flowers, perhaps, for the good of the child and general morale.

They said he was he was lucky, lucky to be alive, but they also were noticing how their own luck had improved. Shortly after his arrival, the miners found new seams of metal in their asteroid, and mining was proceeding at a brisk pace. In short, a boom was on.

The luck was with them, month after month, and they grew prosperous. The boomtown was protective and looked upon strangers with suspicion. Others wanted to come in, drawn by the new prosperity, but they were denied. It was a hermetically sealed world, visited only by traders and resupply transport pilots. Outsiders found it tidy, clean, and sober, a place with girlish frills but no girls at all. They said it was weird, "unnatural" and cultish.

"May we please see the baby?" said the old woman, flanked by her fellow missionaries, a man and a woman. Shoe read the trio like a hand of cards, and saw the opening as a "granny" move.

"No," said Young, sitting behind his office desk. "He's doing fine."

"I'm sure that baby's a ton of trouble," said the male missionary, stepping forward. "We could take him off your hands for you."

"No thank you," said Young.

"He has a name, you know," said Shoe. "It's Tony Jade."

"Ah, jade," said the woman, taking her turn. "Because that's the best Luck, am I right?"

"You got it, sister," said Young.

"My husband erred in trying to make it sound as though we would be doing you a favor in taking Tony Jade," she said. "We humbly request it for the child. The Goddess of Mercy would smile upon such an agreement. This is no place for an infant."

"Now look here," started Young, his face flushing.

"Mr. President, allow me to explain," said Shoe, making like a diplomat. He turned to the outsiders and said, "We acknowledge that our settlement is less than optimal for childrearing. We citizens desire improvements to that end, but only on our terms. I myself lead a majority faction with plans for a hotel with which we could entice one or two good families to immigrate. These families would have women and children, both of obvious benefit for Tony Jade."

"What about the minority faction?" asked the woman, an eager light in her eyes. "What do they want?"

"They want to keep things as they are, at least for a year," said Young. The light in the woman's eyes died, and then he added, "The compromise was a four-month wait."

Then the old woman suddenly dropped to her knees. "We beg you," she said, as the others followed her lead, "in the name of Mercy!"

"Get up!" roared Young. "Get out of here! How dare you! I should have you thrown out—"

"This meeting is over," said Shoe, and he hustled the missionaries out.

When he returned a few minutes later, Young had composed himself.

"Well, that's over," said Shoe, dusting his

hands off.

"See why I made sure that Doc kept Tony away?" asked Young. "That would've been just another way to get their foot in the door."

"Are they gonna stay long?"

"I'll only let them have another day or two."

Shoe stretched, his arms going up and out, his back popping.

"That's the end of my day at the office," he said with contentment. "You ready to quit yet?"

"In a while. I'll meet you at Jin's."

Shoe went out, emerging in the uptown end of the main cave. He clomped along the sidewalk past the dormitory section, past the mining shaft, and came to Jin's Hydroponics. When he walked in, Jin called out, "What's the word, Shoe?"

Before Shoe could answer there was a sudden rumbling sound and a tremor in the floor. Pressure doors automatically slammed shut as someone shouted, "It's a blowout!"

Shoe ran to the window just in time to see a few men sucked out into space through a gaping hole in the sky. None of them were wearing vac suits, and in seconds each died the horrible death that all belters fear.

Then Tony Jade's little pressure cabin was sucked out, too, tumbling end over end.

Shoe jumped into a vac suit and organized a rescue party. They took the little hopper at the space dock and burned up a lot of reaction mass chasing after the cabin through the expanding

plume of debris. The hour it took to match veloci-
ties felt like it lasted a bitter day, followed by an
eternity as they nudged the cabin to halt its rolling.

Shoe went into the cabin's airlock, cheered at
the green light indicators showing there was air
inside. As he agonized through the additional wait
of the airlock cycle, he pounded on the hatch to
send a signal that help was at hand.

Once inside the cabin proper, Shoe saw the
crumpled form of Doc wedged in a corner, battered and bruised, but still holding the Miracle of
Asteroid Camp 88 in his arms. Shoe took off his
helmet. As he bent over the pair, the boy gave a
cry, but Doc himself was dead.

The flight back to the asteroid felt longer, though
it was shorter by the clock.

A commotion in the docking cave died the
moment Shoe the Gambler came in, with tiny
Tony Jade in his arms. In the sudden silence he
asked the nearest man, "What was the fighting
about?"

"Well, uh, you know," stammered the man, un-
able to meet his eyes. "Whose fault the blowout
was."

Shoe sighed.

"The blowout was everybody's fault," he said
to the men. "Here's Tony, our boy. Doc fought to

save him. He succeeded, but gave his life in the process. I'm sure if any one of us had been there, we'd have done the same."

A few men stood taller at that, and some nodded.

"Now, little Tony here, he changed us all, and changed us for the better. We weren't working for ourselves anymore, we were working for him. It may be that our enthusiasm for making the family hotel got the better of us, so that we took chances and got a little careless in the mining."

Shoe heard some muttering, saw some sideways glances.

"But at the same time, blowouts happen. That old pressure hut would've been fine if its anchors had only held out. We failed there, too. There's plenty of blame to go around."

The men grew quiet again.

"Still, we've learned our lesson. So let's not waste any effort beating ourselves, or beating each other. The odds were bad, and we've just been reminded. I say we give him over to the missionaries. It will be the best, and the safest."

All eyes went to Supervisor Young, whose hands were balled into fists that were shaking. He glowered at Shoe, but then the fight went out of him.

"He's right," said Young, his eyes tearing up. "We owe it to him. And we owe it to Doc, since none of us could replace him."

TRIBAL FLYER
JIBRIL

The wind pushed directly against Jibril's body as he flew over the familiar mountains. He sat on the lower wing of his biplane, beside the empty passenger seat. The gasoline engine behind him drove two rear-facing propellers, and the upper wing acted as a roof. An open frame connected the wings to the tail assembly of twin rudders and a stabilizer. Constructed of wood and cloth, the vehicle was like a long-armed box kite sporting a smaller box kite as a tail.

Jibril was on furlough, having finally earned enough money in the scouting service for a bride price. The swollen red sun behind him was the star Joo Tseo, known on ancient charts as "Gliese 693," which hung forever motionless in the sky of its habitable planet.

Jibril crested the last ridge and came upon Pseudopines Park, nestled in the mountains. At the sight of his home village, the fatigue of his two-hour flight vanished, as did his apprehension about the meeting ahead. He turned the steering wheel to point toward Widow Rasha's farm. Widow Rasha was the guardian of his intended, the orphan Buthaynah. If she would accept the bride price, Jibril and Buthaynah could wed.

Hoping for a dramatic entrance, he landed on the farm's dirt road, where the double wheels rolled on the hard-baked surface and the back ends of the landing skids scraped against it. He taxied up to the weather-beaten farmhouse and shut off the engine with a feeling of satisfaction.

Scarce had he removed his leather flying cap when he heard the quarrelsome voice of an old woman, shouting, "What you want?"

She was at a window with a rifle ready. Jibril smiled and raised his hands high.

"Auntie Rasha, it is me, Jibril!" he called. He hopped down from the pilot seat to the ground. "Is —can—may I speak with Buthaynah?"

"Jibril from the village?" she asked. "Jibril the wainwright's boy?"

"Yes, that's right, but now 'Jibril the Flyer.'"

"Oh Jibril, they took her away!"

"Who?" he cried, bristling at the implication of bride-napping, but she had left the window and was hurrying to the front door. During the interval his mind began running through a list of local troublemakers who might be involved, and calculating the ransom they could demand. It would be a fraction of the bride price, and of course he would pay, but how had they known of his intention since it was a secret?

"Who took her?" he demanded as she opened the front door.

"That airship from the Nightlands!"

"What?" he said, stunned at a crime far beyond what he had been thinking.

"She went out to pick berries and they took her away."

"When was this?"

"Just today."

"What time, exactly? I need to know!"

"Oh, will you go rescue her?"

"Yes."

"Your flyer friends, can you call them out like kin?"

"No, I go alone. Please, this is very important. It's past thirteen now—what time was she taken?"

"It was around ten or eleven o'clock."

"Not so long ago! But why were they this far sunward?"

"I don't know."

"I must go now."

"Good luck, and God bless you!"

Jibril flew a few miles to the scout base Maris, where he asked about the airship as the fuel man filled his biplane's gas tank.

"Yeah, that's the *Cloud Queen*," said Haddad. "She had trouble with a couple engines an' got blowed off course. Folk around here never seen

Nightlanders nor stellars before—course, they're all human just like us, only they do look different an' act funny. Anyway, I fiddled with their engines some, sold 'em fuel, and saw them off."

"They left around ten?"

"Mm, closer to eleven. Ten-forty, around that."

Jibril grunted, thinking on how he had been washing and shaving at the time when his intended was being abducted. "Widow Rasha says they took her girl Buthaynah."

"Ya mean, like kidnapping?"

"I call it bride-napping."

"Whoa!" The older man did a double take, sizing him up with new respect. "I didn't know you— she—Well, I didn't see her around here, not at all. Then again, they did buy a lot of foodstuffs from the village. Maybe somebody there knows something."

"No time for that," said Jibril. "How fast can that thing go?"

"They said seventy-five miles per hour was the normal cruising speed, but now, probably half that."

"So forty, you think?" The man nodded. "And they've had three hours since they left, which puts them at a hundred and twenty miles away."

"Heading straight south," said the fueler. He sucked his teeth in concentration. "That would be around Mitra's Grange. Ever been there?" Jibril shook his head. "Well, if our figures are right, you got about twenty miles per hour on them. If you sprint, you might catch them in seven or eight hours. But you can't fly around the clock like they do, so it would have to be in that one sprint."

"Think they might land for repairs?"

"I doubt it. Their Nightland stuff is plenty stellar. But maybe they'll try at an aerodrome, like at Tarafah the Taweel, or at Medicine Hill, them both down by Dinosaur Swamp."

Jibril flew nightward out of the arid highlands, the wind pushing against his body in the familiar way even as he ventured into the unknown. He thought about how, just an hour before, he had entertained a notion of taking Buthaynah on a flight over their village if she said yes to marrying him. Things had changed so fast it was hard to grasp.

He tried to make sense of what few details he had. He supposed that the stellar tourists had seen Buthaynah. Two or more decided to kidnap her. They tricked her, drugged her somehow, and smuggled her onto the airship before it left, hiding her in their cabin. By the time she woke up, they would be hundreds of miles away—perhaps even in the twilight.

Or maybe it went another way—after lifting off from scout base Maris they saw her alone picking berries and dropped down to snatch her. If that were the case, then the captain was in on it. For that matter, a pre-flight kidnapping might have been carried out by Nightlander crewmen rather than stellar passengers.

The last of the mountains fell beneath Jibril, followed by a hundred miles of the Sea of Sand. Just beyond another mountain range, the Kabir Valley opened up with its sunward town Mitra's Grange the centerpiece to a patchwork of farmlands.

Jibril landed at the scout base attached to the small airfield there. Still sitting at his seat, he reached into his leather jacket and drew forth the sealed white envelope that held all of his dreams in the form of twenty-two sols. He hesitated for a moment, then tore it open to use the bride price for rescuing the bride.

The local temperature was around body heat, but low humidity eased the burden, so that it felt sharp and bright. Jibril ate a falafel and studied a map while his biplane was refueled, then took to the air again, flying in the direction to which the permanent shadows pointed.

The valley ended with gentle hills so soft and rounded as to seem the hips of women lying beneath a blanket of golden yellow velvet. Jibril aimed toward a smoky haze in the distance, the smog of Bituman. As he neared the coalmining town, the landscape became as pitted and scarred as a plundered tomb, a miniature version of the sunward coalfields fought over by empires, the hotlands where Jibril served.

Bituman featured a middling airfield where Jibril landed, refueled, and set out again. The coal-fields petered out to a long series of hills and dales, east/west valleys where one side had perpetual sunlight and the other was in constant shade. The hills at last gave way to a reddishwood forest marching majestically to the edge of Dinosaur Swamp.

At this point, six hours into the chase, Jibril could see the shiny zeppelin moving slowly over the vast swamp, but he was nearly out of fuel. He landed at Tarafah the Taweel's aerodrome. When he asked about conditions at Medicine Hill, they told him to watch out for pterodons nesting around there. He bought another falafel for a couple of dinkits, mindful of the cost. He ate the sandwich as they fed his biplane twelve gallons of gasoline and topped off the radiator. After paying two sols and five dinkits for the fuel, he took off.

Jibril caught up with the zeppelin flying slow and low, three hundred and thirty feet over the swamp. Closer up it was a metallic silver, as if sheathed in some stellar metal that was as light as cloth, yet stronger than steel. Jibril was glad to be pacing the *Cloud Queen*, but she was heading south, into the thickest part of the swamp, rather than south by southeast toward Medicine Hill. This meant she would not be landing anytime soon, which spoiled his plan of confronting the kidnappers at an airfield.

He ground his teeth in frustration at being so close and yet still so far from his goal. Then he came up with a scheme.

He gained altitude until he was above the airship, and increased his speed to close with it. He could tell it was more than seven hundred feet long, which was certainly long enough for his purpose, but the curve of the sides meant that only a narrow strip at the top was near level.

Like trying to land on a hotlander sidewalk, he thought, but then he amended this. *No, no, like landing on a bowed country road, and I've done that plenty of times.*

He brought his plane down closer. The gusty crosswind from the left proved challenging, pushing him off the line he was aiming for. He leaned into the wind to correct, but then the wind let off so he moved too far in that direction.

He was ten feet from the zeppelin and the air was still, holding its breath just as he was. He was five feet from the shiny skin and a sudden gust pushed the plane over to the sloping side.

Jibril saw a silver hill rising beside him on the left, nearly brushing his wing with a dangerous kiss. He jerked the steering wheel toward the slope. One landing wheel made contact. Jibril goosed the throttle and drove up the hill.

With a quick fishtail he was on target, so he throttled down.

Jibril was thrown into the steering wheel, just like a time when he had accidentally landed in mud.

He killed the engine, but the airplane, with a

mind of its own, wanted to lift off. He jammed the controls to keep it down. Looking under the wing he sat on, he saw that the wheels had sunken into deep gouges in the airship's cloth fabric. The sled rails of the landing carriage were holding the plane up on one of the metal rings that formed the zeppelin's ribcage.

As he wrestled with the bucking biplane, a group of crewmen spilled out of a hatch ahead, whooping with surprise and alarm.

"Hey Mister Scout, you landed that here?" cried one. "I can't believe it."

"Come help me," said Jibril. "Tie it down, somehow, or just hold it down for a while. I won't be long staying here."

"How much that thing weigh?"

"Right now, around nine hundred pounds."

"Joo Tseo, good thing we're running light. What're you here for?"

"It's important. I need to see the captain."

"Believe me, the captain wants to see *you*."

After a few minutes the plane was secure.

"This way," said the airman.

Jibril followed the man to the hatch and down a ladder stretching for a hundred and twenty feet between the giant helium gas cells. They ended up in the freight section, a platform suspended by metal scaffolding with gas cells to starboard and port.

"There's a party going on right now, Mister Scout ... ?"

"Jibril."

"Scout Jibril, I'm Airman Farad, pleased to meet you. I'll follow you forward, straight to meet the captain at the party."

"He's not in the piloting gondola?" asked Jibril as they started walking.

"No sir, not for a social function like this."

After a few steps in silence, Farad said, "That was sure some landing you made."

"Thanks."

"I guess your business with the captain can't be trusted to the wireless, eh?"

Jibril said nothing, but inside he was chagrined that he had not even considered that such an advanced aircraft would have a wireless radio communication station onboard.

They passed through a portal and walked through the slightly less spartan supplies section. Jibril felt Farad's eyes on his back, and then realized why he was in front—it was not in deference to a guest, it was in suspicion of a presumed thief. He gritted his teeth and said nothing. They passed through a doorway into the passenger area, turned left, and entered a sudden crush of people.

Jibril was stunned. For such a titanic vessel, the passenger area was surprisingly small. The dining room was not ten feet longer than the thirty-nine-foot wingspan of his airplane, and at around twelve feet wide, only twice the width of its wings. There was also a promenade by the big glass windows looking downward, but that added little.

All in all, the size of a classroom or a tavern.

Packed with fifty or sixty people.

And what strange people they seemed to Jibril! Their clothing was exotic to his eyes, interstellar in cut and material. He knew that tourists came from different stars, like Peacock, Hydra, Tucan, and Ara, but he could not tell them apart. All had skins tanned by suns brighter than an M3.5 dwarf. The males wore outfits that were merely bizarre, whereas the females had garb that was shockingly immodest. Jibril absently rubbed his jaw, and became aware of his own sweaty, grimy aroma in a strong contrast to the clean perfume of the tourists.

"Captain?" said his guide, touching his forelock to a gray-bearded man in an impressive uniform of military design.

"Report, Farad."

"Seems, sir, that a scout flyer biplane was landed upon the top, near as right on frame seven."

"Damage to the gas cells?"

"Near minimum, if you can believe it. Got a patch on a few leaks. Fabric's torn, but we can't deal with that until the biplane is away."

"Thank you, Farad." The Captain turned to Jibril.

Farad coughed. "Jibril, this is Captain Malik. Captain, this is Tribal Flyer Jibril."

"What is this all about, Jibril?"

"Bride-napping, sir."

The captain and his airman both paled and took a step back.

"'Bride-napping'?" said the captain.

"Yes, sir," said Jibril. "Someone on this airship, passenger or crew, has taken the orphan Buthaynah from Pseudopines Park, sir." He rested one hand on his holster and the other on his sheathed knife. "I won't leave without her, and I will kill anyone who tries to stop me. Sir."

"It's the girl!" said Farad. "I knew there'd be trouble!"

"Farad, find 'the girl' and bring her here." The captain turned to Jibril. "I believe we can quickly resolve this problem. In the meantime, my airship has been damaged through your reckless behavior."

"My bride was stolen, sir."

"Hmm, yes. Perhaps. Now then, you own your plane?"

"No sir."

"But you know what it is worth?"

"Yes, sir, it's four thousand sols, or two hundred pounds of silver."

"This vessel is considerably more than that."

"And do you own it, sir?"

"Of course not. In fact, my government subsidizes it."

"Congratulations, sir."

Malik looked at him askance, as if to determine with a piercing gaze whether Jibril was a simpleton or a smart alec. "I take it you work at the frontlines?"

"Sometimes, sir. When scouting, sir."

"Isn't that all that a scout does?"

"No sir, there's also courier work, and transportation of officers."

"Here she is, captain," said Farad, drawing a young woman by the wrist.

"Buthaynah!" said Jibril, but then his hand went to his holster. "Don't touch her."

"Jibril?" said Buthaynah, bewildered. She was dressed in exotic clothing, but Jibril was relieved to see it was the modest design of a military type —dainty hat, a jacket with epaulettes and brass buttons, and a knee-length skirt of simple straight lines. She might be an administrator in charge of nurses at a field hospital.

"I've followed this airship for many miles," he said, "tracked it from our homeland, to rescue you."

"But I—"

"Come with me," he said. "My biplane is just on top. Once there, we will be away in an instant."

"Young miss," said the captain. "Do you know this man?"

"Yes, captain sir," she said. "He is Jibril of the village, the wainwright's son."

"*Flyer* Jibril," said Jibril.

"Is he your fiancé?"

"Oh no sir, captain-sir!"

"Only now do I have the bride-price," said Jibril. He dropped to one knee and held up the disheveled white envelope, causing a stir among the passengers. "Buthaynah, I have loved you with all my heart since we were little children. For you I joined the service and worked hard, so that I might be worthy of you. Will you please marry me?"

"*Jibril,*" she said, hand to her blushing cheek. "This is, this is so much, all at once."

"If she was not your fiancée," said the captain, "then your claim of bride-napping has no basis in fact."

"She was taken! Her aunt said so!"

"Wait, wait!" said Buthaynah, gasping for breath. "Jibril, I—I left on my own."

"What?" said Jibril, stunned. "Why?"

"That place was like a prison to me. I had to get out."

"I thought she treated you well."

"Not just the farm, but the village, too. There was nothing for me there. I thought I could find something better somewhere else."

"But the *Nightlands!*" said Jibril. "You would be polluted. Even now you are tainted, but it doesn't matter to me. Let's just get out now."

"No," she said, folding her arms. "I stand by my decision. I won't quit."

Slowly he rose up. "You ran away without telling your auntie, is that it?"

"I told her. I thought she knew. She probably just wants that money from you, and that's part of what I'm trying to get away from."

"I see."

"*She* tricked you, *I* didn't."

"So what is it?" With slitted eyes he glanced around. "Is there some man here for you?"

"No!" she said, her cheeks red. "I have a job, to pay my way."

Jibril sighed heavily, then took off his parachute and held it toward her.

"Here," he said, his tongue thick. "Take it."

"What?" she said, blinking rapidly. "But *why?*"

"You might need it," he said. "If not, then you can sell it in the Nightlands. My gift to you."

He tossed the parachute, forcing her to catch it.

"But you need it," she said.

"I'll get another one."

"I don't even know how to use it."

"It's easy," he told her, glad for a change of subject. "You just put it on, jump clear, and pull the chord." He turned to leave and said, "Goodbye, Buthaynah" over his shoulder before pushing his way through the crowd, back the way he had come.

He passed into the supplies section and found Farad was following him.

"That's rough luck," said the airman.

Jibril glanced back and saw Farad wore a grimace of commiseration that seemed sincere. Jibril said nothing and continued walking, his footsteps heavy.

"Listen, the captain will probably try to put a

lien on you, you know, make you pay for the damages to the ship."

"How can he do that?"

"He knows your name and your village."

"Oh. Of course."

"But hey, maybe I can take up a collection to pay for it. Some of the passengers were talking about it already."

"It doesn't matter. If Buthaynah is not mine, then money doesn't matter."

"Well, maybe tomorrow you'll see it different."

Jibril walked along, numb. He felt a fool, publicly shamed, and yet deep down he had new concerns.

It was a long climb back up to the top of the airship. When he emerged he was pushed by the wind, surprised at how quickly he had grown accustomed to the still air inside. He got onto his biplane and started the engine. The airmen watched closely, and when he signaled they released the wings, allowing the biplane to lift straight up and fly.

But instead of heading back toward the motionless sun, Jibril raced ahead toward the Nightlands.

He used up most of his fuel getting to the nearest airfield, where he bought more gasoline. He had spent nearly a third of the money on the chase. A replacement parachute was out of the question —he had never had that much.

Jibril had flown south about six hundred miles that day, crossing from one climate band to another. That was eight hours of the chase in addition to the couple hours before, amounting to ten hours.

He was fatigued, getting clumsy with his hands and fuzzy with his thoughts. Now that his vehicle was prepared, his own physical stamina became a weak link. But he was certain of two things—that, one way or another, this would be the last leg of his chase, and that Buthaynah did not yet know about the world outside their village.

He lay on his back on the ground beside his biplane, forcing himself to rest. He sipped cold tea from a canteen as he watched the sky. The weather was muggy, with humidity from the swamp making it feel heavy and dull. Joo Tseo was alarmingly low to the north.

After a while the airship *Cloud Queen* came into view. As it passed he checked his watch. The little arm pointing up to 24, the long arm pointing down to 12—it was zero thirty, the middle of the witching hour. A new day had begun.

He rose, stretched, performed some calisthenics. He buckled on his flying cap, wound the scarf around his neck. He started the engine, lowered his goggles, and took to the air once more.

Jibril quickly caught up with the zeppelin and then kept a steady distance of about a half-mile behind it. The droning of the engine to his right was hypnotic. He sang songs to himself in an attempt to fight off the fatigue dragging down his eyelids.

Jibril thought of the hotlands, and the cities he had seen there. Once beautiful, they were now broken by war—domes like shattered eggshells, graceful spires shivered in two, palatial gardens ruined by neglect and abuse. Worse still were the fallen women who lived there like ghouls, renting their bodies to whichever army happened to occupy the place.

Buthaynah knew nothing of this. She only knew that the village rules imprisoned her, and she dreamed that outside the village, away from the mountains, she would be free.

She probably didn't know that their hill-ways had a reputation reaching far beyond the Sea of Sand—that the hill-men were seen as violent thieves always feuding, whereas the hill-women were untouchable.

So she had been protected by this reputation, as if surrounded by an invisible shield. But it was only a matter of time until some man laid hand on her, and when he did, she would have to make a choice.

A small speck dropped from the big silver airship, snapping Jibril from his pondering. He shook his head and blinked, wondering, and then the speck sent up a tendril that blossomed into a white parachute. His heart leapt with joy and relief at the sight.

He slowed down, made a wide circle around her. The ground below was relatively flat and clear, with a river flowing north, back toward the swamp. He licked his lips, imagining the sweetest kiss would soon be his.

She landed in a heap. He brought his biplane down to land about thirty feet from her. After he killed the engine he whipped off his cap as he rushed toward her.

"That was terrible!" she cried, her steps unsteady as she dragged the parachute behind her.

"That was perfect!" said Jibril. "You hurt your leg? But you can stand! And walk!"

"No," she insisted, "it was scary, very scary!" She suddenly clutched her sides and shivered violently. "Th-this is a-a-all your f-fault! Things were g-going *fine* until y-y-you showed up!"

"Now wait, just wait," he said, trying to shape his sudden angry confusion into soothing words. "You've just come down in a parachute. It's very upsetting, the first time. You should sleep, and tomorrow things—"

"That guy put his hand up my skirt and the captain just laughed!"

Buthaynah's hands flew to her mouth, as if she could take back what she had just blurted out. Jibril found himself looking at his boot, thinking murderous thoughts.

She broke the heavy silence by choking out a request: "Take me to an inn."

Jibril glanced at her, looked around at points

on the horizon, and considered for a moment. "I didn't see anything like that around here," he said.

"Take me in that aeroplane to a town, then."

"No. We're sleeping here. Under the airplane."

"Not together!"

"No! Of course not! You will be between the wheels, and I will be to one side. Look, we will use your parachute to make a tent there for you."

He gathered up the white silk and arranged it in the two-foot gap between the lower wing and the ground, laughing inside at his earlier notions of kisses, but still genuinely happy at how things had turned out. This task complete, he took his bedroll and spread it out below the wingtip, about fifteen feet away.

"All right," he said as he lay down. "You're all set. Go to sleep now. We have a lot of travel ahead tomorrow."

She lingered, looking around.

"The sky sure is different here," she said. "So orange."

"Yes it is. They call it 'sunset,' I've heard."

"The sun looks different, too."

"Yes."

"How can that be?"

"I don't know."

"And it's warmer than home! Why is that, when we are closer to the night?"

"Elevation," said Jibril with a weary sigh. "Mitra's Grange is twelve degrees hotter than home. This is nothing."

"But—"

"Go to bed. We'll talk about it in the morning. I promise."

She paused for a moment.

"Good sleeping, Jibril. And thank you. For everything."

It was like a kiss, maybe even better, and with a smile on his lips, Jibril fell fast asleep.

GENRE PURGE 3

Accidents happen, and no one is more aware of this fact than the personnel of a bustling spaceport. But not all accidents are equal: an old kerosene-fueled V-2 Rocket Cargo Ship suffering a 'malf' is nothing compared to an atomic-powered Kiwi or Nerva. The former might destroy a single family house in rocket town; the latter would wipe out an entire block.

"DOWNRANGE" BY JOSEPH ANKRUM

C old shock crackled through Arthur Penman the moment he realized a genre purge had begun. The TV continued the Second Manhattan Show Trial broadcast live from Boswash, but he was numb. It was too early for a purge, by four years at least. Another alarming surprise was that the genre upper tier was getting hammered again, when it seemed in fairness that the lower tier was due a drubbing.

Arthur hurried from his one-room at the repurposed Polywater Institute toward Kafobutiko, the usual shop for genre workers to meet. His mind was racing with the history of genre purges:

at age thirty, he had been a member of the genre union for eleven years, having joined after the first purge.

Arriving at the grimy utilitarian coffee shop he spotted Otto Wright, whose bewildered expression spoke volumes. Arthur made his way among the small tables to where owlish Otto sat.

"I guess it's true, then?" he asked.

"But it's too soon," said Otto. The gap between first and second purges had been eight years; and furthermore, this was not even an election year. "It's crazy—it makes no sense."

Arthur dropped into the chair across from his friend and said, "What's crazy is slamming the elites so hard, since the newbies deserve a spanking."

Into the shop burst their colleagues Quill and Spill.

"We are all Venusians now," said Quill.

"What do you mean?" said Arthur.

"There," said Spill, pointing to the TV screen showing live coverage of the Trial. An elite editor was confessing to corruption of youth, promotion of wage-slavery, and the propagation of pseudo-science by falsely promoting the Dean Drive. More importantly, he was the heart and face of the Mars project.

"*Downrange* is finished," said Otto, his voice hollow.

"What?" said Arthur. "But—that's our careers! Most of it, anyway."

"Content shift," said Otto with a defeated shrug.

The four sat there in silence. Arthur's heart ached over the last three years of work being suddenly erased. The writers of the Mars project were entrusted with visualizing the coming reality, and with gusto they had taken to describing the heroic trailblazing, the conquest of space. In their shared future history, the early days of V-2 rocket cargo ships gave way to the boom era featuring atomic rockets with their "downrange" hazards of exhaust and crashes. Theirs were tales of romance and adventure in the Martian bases as well as Earth's "rocket towns," where neighborhoods around the spaceport were rated for radiation hazard in terms of "cigarettes per day." Stories of hard-working men, unforgiving environments, and the hardships of frontier living.

In stark contrast to the Venus group, which seemed to be all about easy terraforming of the sister world by bacteria, overseen by bald women in swimsuits onboard orbital stations.

"Well," said Otto, "how many stories you got out?"

"Ten—no, twelve. Do you think I could place an Adam 'n' Eve over at *Orbita*?"

Otto scoffed, shook his head.

The others reported similar numbers, then Otto urged them to get coffee.

Following the other two, Arthur dutifully went to the counter, handed over his ration booklet, and got a small cup of civet coffee. Back at the table he sipped and grimaced.

"Civet poop was better before the first purge."

"Sure," said Otto. "The old elites had the real stuff."

Along came a trio of genre-workers named Baboo, Teller, and Quinn the Mex. Being young they knew only the second purge, so their elders gave them the info dump:

The first purge came after a national election where the One Party triumphed over the Other Party. There were two big changes that time: the lower level members, around ten percent of the union, were kicked out for being non-professional; and the so-called Scandinavian Model, or "ScanMod," was instituted whereby the State was compelled to buy stories from the writers. This period was considered a "Golden Age."

Then the group discussed Genre Purge 2, where there was another election turnover allowing the Other Party back into power. That was the time the award-winning authors and editors, something like eighteen percent of the union, were kicked out for being stooges of the One Party; and ScanMod was replaced with the National Patron, or "NatPat," in which various governmental groups commissioned work on specific topics and themes.

The seven colleagues shared the news, commiserated, and pledged to help each other during the shifting circumstances now thrust upon them.

Then the party broke up as each hurried off to manage his affairs in this new crisis.

The street Arthur pushed his way through seemed normal, a typical day in the Midwestern end of chain-city Chipitts. It seemed the news had not yet trickled out to the general public. There were the usual lines at shops, rather than the long lines of a panic. The local slidewalk was motionless due to breakage or strike, and Arthur noticed a new monocycle repair shop. His heart lifted at the prospect of taking his non-functional single-wheel motorized riding vehicle in for repair, thereby freeing himself from unreliable mass transit. But that smacked of elitism, which brought him back to pondering purges.

Exile, labor camp, and prison were the typical punishments handed out at a purge; but by the same token, there was advancement for some, or perhaps a few at least.

Wrapped in such thought, too late he recognized he had stepped into a trouble zone: what appeared to be a lackluster protest demonstration at a Dean Drive lab. Before he could duck away, a riot policeman spotted him and shouted, "Citizen, does this look like a riot to you? Do your duty, and show them how it is done!"

Chagrined, Arthur stepped forward, hoping to take up one of the bricks set out on the card table, but another cop thrust a lit gasoline bomb into his hand instead, and Arthur gave it everything. This inspired or shamed the proles into action, and as the cops applauded, Arthur slipped away.

Back in his one-room at the Polywater he made a call to the office of *Orbita*. He was on hold for about an hour, then suddenly he was face to face with an editor.

"Sorry to be bothering you . . . "

"It's all right," said the editor. "What have you got?"

"It's an Adam 'n' Eve—"

"Oh no—"

"—set on Venus."

"On Venus, huh?"

"Yes!"

"Is it cyano or rhodo?"

"What's that?"

"The bacteria," said the editor. "For the terra-forming. It is either the one or the other, the blue or the red."

"Oh," said Arthur, vaguely recalling that one was faster than the other, theoretically completing the process in years rather than decades. "Well, whichever you prefer."

"I like it! Okay, so how does it end?"

"He says, 'Madam of Venus, I'm—'"

"'Uranus'!"

"Huh?" said Arthur.

"That's how this will work, we will get in a story that mocks the old way."

"Okay, so it's, 'Madam of—'"

"'Maiden.' Make it 'maiden.'"

"'Maiden of Venus, I'm from Uranus.'"

"No, not 'from.' Just 'I'm Uranus.'"

"Uh, okay."

"Great. It practically writes itself. Send it in ASAP."

"The V-2 Rocket Cargo Ship was going wacky, that typical problem with the gyros. Rookie Jay Burt was the only man who could do anything about it, and there were only two methods available: he could try to fly the crippled craft by wire to crash safely in an uninhabited area; or he could hit the self-destruct button and let the debris fall where it would, downrange." ("Downrange" by Joseph Ankrum)

Four months into the purge came an unexpected turn as pounding began against the lower tier. For the first time both upper and lower tiers were being flushed out simultaneously. And the penalties were harsher than ever: exile was not an option; labor camps and prison were the mild form; mental hospitals and fat farms were the worst. This put Big Fear into Mid Tier.

Arthur put in a call to Otto Wright, now an editor at a new magazine.

"I am eager to write," said Arthur, "but it is difficult these days."

"These are challenging times, to be sure."

"I think I could write a Mars story set on Venus—"

"Avoid Venus until the blue/red thing works itself out," said Otto, referencing the factional fight that had broken out in the Venus group. "Set it on an orbital station, no terraforming."

"All right, it is on an orbital. Still, there are all sorts of options. How about a story where a quick-thinking expert deals with a crisis?"

"That seems elitist," said Otto. "Better if it is a problem that an average woman could solve without any help."

"Okay, how about heroic action, by a woman, in responding to an accident?"

"Well, but there are no accidents in a scientific utopia. So it must be sabotage by mutants."

Arthur suppressed a shudder at the mention of "mutants." This recent trend in scapegoating had led to an appalling number of genre workers being convicted on fabricated charges. "Mutants" were routinely blamed for sabotaging slidewalks, causing food shortages, and any of the other many problems affecting Boswash, Chipitts, and Sansan.

"I envision these sweating men with tools—"

"No, no, no," said Otto with eye-rolling fatigue. "That's the Mars thing again. Unless they are sweating mutants. What we need are international women with purple hair and silver jumpsuits, cool and competent, sitting at computer stations."

"You can see how hard this is for me," said Arthur. "It is like all the rules have changed."

"They have changed. Genre is now a kind of comfort food."

"Comfort food?" Arthur choked. He held back a rant, a full blown idiot lecture about how genre workers had been like unto a priesthood delivering the vision that precedes existence; how they had brain-strained to provide the direction and drive to the entire scientific/industrial complex, giving rise to whole new sectors of the economy, the very dreams our stuff is made of, from television to vidphones, from slidewalks to monocycles, from fission power to the promise of fusion power. He managed to distill this down and, after passing it through a filter against elitism, he said, "It used to be visionary escapism, channeling the spirit of adventure."

"Now that people are losing jobs—and worse —the official line is that the fantasy should be about safe situations."

There was an awkward moment of silence. Arthur grew desperate to say something, anything, that might give him an edge.

"Too bad about Quinn the Mex," he blurted, referring to their colleague recently sentenced to twenty years at a fat farm.

"Who?"

"Quinn the—"

"Shh," hissed Otto, his face a mask of fearful rage. "This is monitored. Don't forget your part in his fate!"

"My part? I had—"

"Sounds great!" said Otto, now beaming false enthusiasm. "I look forward to seeing it. Send it ASAP."

"Wiping the sweat from his eyes, Jay Burt knew this was his last chance, an opportunity to fix those two failures in one go, or fumble again and see his town go up in atomic fire." ("Downrange" by Joseph Ankrum)

After nineteen months, the fever of the purge had run its course. Like most, Arthur now had several jobs, one of which was senior editor at a new magazine. In his corner office at the Crony Building he went through dozens of vidphone pitches from genre workers.

The mind-numbing drudgery of the work was wearing him out. To counter this he kept reminding himself of the Lodge meeting scheduled for that night. Mostly he thought of the coffee. Then came a call that upset his equilibrium:

"Thank you for taking my call."

"Yes, yes. What have you got for me?"

"How about a fictional treatment of the third genre purge?"

"Huh," said Arthur, knocked out of his grump

by this kick to the gut.

"Too soon?"

"Seems a bit vague," said Arthur, trying for abstraction by looking off toward the upper wall. "It's hard to get the whole sweep of history in a short story. Too dry—you need characters, and that limits things, scope."

"I thought it could focus on one man, like Otto Wright, and follow his path through the courts to the mutant camps—"

"I think you are right," said Arthur, "it is too soon, too confrontational."

The other was clearly getting desperate.

"It could be set on the Moon. Say there are these five friends, and each betrays the other—"

"Do not call this magazine again," said Arthur. "I'm warning you."

He ended the call and quit work early in an angry haze. At his car he realized it was too soon to head for the Lodge, so he settled on a visit to one of his stables.

He drove across town to a shabby district where slouched a boarded-up cold fusion research lab. Hidden within this crumbling edifice was a two-room workshop where others crafted genre that went out under his name.

When he entered the place the old guy in the corner looked up for a moment then went back to marking a manuscript, while the two youngsters lounging at the kitchen table did a quick double-take.

"You're early," said one newbie.

"Yeah," growled Arthur. "Spot inspection. How's the work going?"

"Ahead of schedule."

"That's good, 'cause here's a new one for you. Top priority. There's this muckraker, see? And he starts trying to embarrass the government over recent security decisions. He acts like he is going to expose a scandal, but then it turns out that the whole thing is dreamed up, and paid for, by filthy mutants. Justice prevails."

"Great stuff, boss."

"It writes itself."

The old guy in the corner set down the manuscript and stood up to stretch.

"Might I have a word?" he said to Arthur. "Alone?"

"Yeah, sure. You two relax in the bunkroom for a few minutes."

As the newbies left, Arthur said, "How's the novel coming?"

"It's all right," said the elder, shrugging. "But I'm wondering about getting rehabilitated. You said—"

"It is still very dangerous," said Arthur. "I know everybody is saying the purge is over, they're giddy with it, but I'm telling you there is still a lot of danger for an unperson like you."

"But you said—"

"Look, Ankrum, I know what I said, all right? Only it's not so easy as that. I saved your life—will you agree that is true?"

"Yes, of course."

"Okay. Well now it goes the other way—if you pop up too early, not only do they liquidate you, but they also get me, right? It isn't just your life anymore, in fact it never was—it's my life, too."

"I just don't know how much longer I can go on like this," said Ankrum. "I feel the walls closing in on me—I'm hungry all the time—"

"Be patient. Just—"

"I want some *real* food. All this crap, this space food junk—krill paste, food pills, liquid breakfast, soylent crackers—it's wearing me down."

"It has kept you alive."

"It's all expired!"

"That's how I was able to get it for you through the black market," said Arthur. "It is no longer counted. And it isn't cheap, either."

"But it's not fit for human consumption, either, if it ever was."

"Just a little longer. When it's over it will all seem so short a time, so long ago. Here, I'll take the novel now, as is."

"Are you sure?"

"Yes," said Arthur. "You deserve a break. And I'll work on getting you some better food, okay?"

"That would be good."

"Hang in there. I'm working on it, you know I am. For both of us."

That would have been a perfect moment to leave, but it was still too early for the Lodge. In order to kill time, Arthur asked the newbies to show their work. The results made him apoplectic.

"This is what you call 'ahead of schedule'? What a stupid lie. And the quality is abysmal. People with five times your talent have been sent to prison, whereas those with only three times your talent have been liquidated."

He hit them, he stomped around, he pounded the table. Then he had them go through a self-criticism session. This done, he berated them as they outlined the new muckraker story.

Finally it was time to leave, and he drove off with some small satisfaction.

For an hour he drove from the city into the dustbowl, while the twilight deepened to hide all signs of entropy and decay: the failed hydroponic farms and ostrich ranches; the mile-wide dish of the rectenna; the wireless power transmission towers; the weather-control cloudscrapers. When he pulled into the driveway of the Lodge his headlights showed the other two cars were already there, a good sign. Once he shut off his vehicle he could make out the faint light from oil lamps and candles coming through the cabin's windows.

He went inside to form the local triumvirate with Enigma and Cipher.

Following the rules, their conversation during the meal was all fairly light and inconsequential. But after they had removed the dishes it was time for business.

Most of the items on the agenda were boilerplate: facts (that were dubious), figures (that were fraudulent), rumors (assumed to be true), and trends.

As they were finishing up, Arthur mentioned the problematic pitch he had received during his workday, naming the offending genre worker. He told them in meticulous detail, ending with, "This is very serious. Something must be done."

"I don't know," said Cipher. "Maybe it is just a joke."

Arthur stiffened. He had not thought of that.

"You make my point," he said. "It would be bad enough if this sophomoric scribbler is acting on his own. But think how much worse it would be if he is repeating a line fed to him by another faction. They are probing me; they are testing us. Is it only a tease?"

The others shook their heads. There was no such thing as a tease.

"It is a threat," said Enigma. "Still, we are under pressure to produce an elite."

"Is it a quota?"

"Hardly," said Cipher. "It is the work that must be done. Like taking out the garbage."

Arthur considered his thumbnail for a moment, running through the options. He decided.

"I will give you an elite in exchange for the silencing of the muckraker."

"Some low-level elite," said Enigma.

"The soul of *Downrange*," said Arthur.

"Interesting!" said Cipher.

"But only if he gets a mild sentence," said Arthur. "Exile. Yes, exile to a civet ranch."

"I think that can be arranged."

"The muckraker deserves the harsh sentence," said Arthur.

"Naturally," said Enigma. "Please jot down the address of your elite and I will see to it immediately."

As Arthur wrote, he voiced additional thoughts.

"There are a couple newbies at the place. They should be left alone, unless they do anything really stupid."

"I understand," said Enigma, taking the bit of paper. "Well, then, I'll get going."

Now that the work was done, the remaining two had their coffee. Arthur looked back on a productive day: two problems liquidated, even though he had made a point of leniency. When he took the first sip, he sighed with childlike happiness.

"That's the real Civet," he said. "Best stuff on Earth."

Cipher agreed.

"Jay Burt's skill had held out, this time. There was always next time, until there wasn't. This was life on the edge, a place where a man should risk it all or get out of the ring." ("Downrange" by Joseph Ankrum)

BEYOND THE
STARRY TEMPEST

"One A.U. out," reported lieutenant Roger Thom, the new first mate. "We're clear now."

"That's . . . your homeworld, Rachel," said Commander Les Kennedy to the sole survivor of the doomed outpost.

Nineteen-year-old Rachel Morbin stared in mute horror at the image on the main screen. Thom started counting down from fifteen.

The ordeal of the last few days reminded Kennedy of the war. Looking onto Rachel's blonde loveliness beside him, he felt wonder at the innocence that radiated from her with the beauty of a snowflake, fragile and ephemeral. She had been born and raised on a world so isolated that she had no concept of the interstellar conflict that had left continents radioactive during her lifetime. Barnard's Star was just a star to her, not the site of a treacherous invasion from colonies at Ross 154.

The planet Altair Five exploded with a dazzling flash. Rachel cried out and buried her face against his chest. He said soothing things about her father, about the posthumous laurels he would receive for discovering the extinct Forerunners. Then he took her to his cabin and proposed.

It was a wedding in hyperspace, presided over by the bosun, who, at 31, was the oldest on the ship.

Kennedy waited at the makeshift altar with Thom beside him as best man.

"You're all set for the next year of shipboard life," said Thom out of the side of his mouth.

"I hope it will last longer than that," said Kennedy, straightening up to his full six feet of height.

The twelve other crewmen of the cruiser had formed two columns with a short aisle between. Appearing at the end of the aisle was Rachel, on the arm of Rob, her unique robot.

Cook played the wedding march on his harmonica, cueing robot and bride to walk forward. All Rachel knew about human social interaction came from books and library movies—luckily she knew about weddings this way. Rob, the seven-foot tall metal man, had been built by the late professor using Forerunner technology. It was as incredible to the Earthmen as a genie, yet it was a gentle giant.

"The girls will weep when they hear the news," murmured Thom. "I'm thinking of a certain governor's daughter on Alpha C . . ."

"Aim high," said Kennedy with a smile and a twinkle in his blue eyes. But as the robot delivered the bride, Kennedy wondered how he could explain recent history to Rachel. How he had enlisted, fought at Barnard's, then Ross 154, and finally Epsilon Indi. She knew about aliens, the only aliens mankind had discovered—how could he tell her about humanity?

"Ahem," said the bosun, standing with his back to the astrogation globe that dominated the center of the small, circular bridge. "Let's—hm, *let us* begin.

"Shipmates and passengers, we are gathered here—"

Collision klaxons interrupted him. The spacemen rushed to their stations around the astrogation globe.

"It's a ship, sir," said Thom, looking at the scope. "A big one, right on us."

"Evasive maneuvers," said Kennedy, standing behind him. "On screen."

"Aye-aye, sir," said both Lt. Ritchie at the helm and Thom at the scope.

The main screen lit up, showing a ship of triangular shape with nacelles on the two stern corners. It was at least ten times the size of their saucer, and an open cargo bay gaped near its center.

"No good, they're taking us in," said Ritchie.

"Landing field on, full flux."

"Aye-aye."

Frightened, Rachel slipped into the shelter of the captain's arms, her head against his shoulder. A shudder went through the ship as it touched down within the alien cargo bay.

"Landing field off," said Kennedy. "Landing strut down."

"Aye-aye," said Ritchie.

"Signal coming in," said Thom. "On screen now."

The picture showed a fuzzy sequence of strange shapes. A voice spoke in unknown languages.

"What do you make of that?" said Kennedy.

"Is it some kind of Rosetta Stone?" said Linstrom.

"'Curdle,'" said Rachel, turning to Rob. "Did I read that?"

"I believe 'bent' or 'warp' would be more accurate, miss," said Rob. "It is a warning of some—"

Then came a chaotic ripping of space that tossed them all around as if they were beads in a baby's rattle.

Rachel woke up on the deck. She sat up with effort, her blue eyes squinting while she felt her head for injuries. "What happened?" She looked around at the men beginning to stir from the floor around her.

"I don't know," said Ritchie, leaning on the helm. "It felt like we went through trans-light without being in the tubes."

"Where is the captain?" she said.

"He's not here," said Thom, limping over from behind the astrogation globe. "Not on the ship."

"The robot is having a seizure," said the bosun to Rachel. "Maybe you can help."

"Mr. Thom, there's something coming through," said Ritchie. "I'll put it on the main screen."

Kennedy woke with a flinch, and jumped up to face the emergency. He was shocked to find himself in a large gray room rather than in his ship.

Three robed aliens stood before him: a gray humanoid with bulging head, a robot built like a large flightless bird, and a plant-man with four stubby legs and leaves for hair.

"Who are you?" he said, finding his voice. "Where's my ship?"

"We are your judges," said the humanoid. "Your ship is safe."

"Where is this place?"

"This is our ship," said the plant-man.

"Commander Kennedy," said the gray humanoid, "you stand accused of planetary destruction and of stealing Forerunner knowledge. How do you plead?"

"Under what authority do you hijack a United Space Starship and hold us prisoner?" demanded Kennedy. "Who are you?"

"We are concerned neighbors from the local community, called by a warpspace beacon in the Altair system," said the humanoid.

"We are your technological superiors," said the robot.

"You are strangers to us," said the plant-man. "We are your judges."

"Again I ask, how do you plead?" said the humanoid.

"I'm innocent of the charges," said Kennedy. "I lost several men at Altair Five, including my astrogator and my ship's surgeon, but I didn't destroy the planet. Professor Morbin did that."

"Your ship left the planet, with the only survivors and witnesses," said the plant-man.

"That's true," said Kennedy. "My mission was to rescue the colonists."

"You are the captain of the ship," said the robotic one. "What happened there is your responsibility."

Kennedy considered for a moment. "I understand."

"Good," said the gray humanoid, giving a tilt of its head. "Your trial begins now."

The screen went blank.

"We have to get him!" said Rachel.

"We leave him," said first mate Thom. "Ship and crew come first."

"He's my—"

"He would want me to save you, too."

"But—"

"I'm in command." He turned away. "Science team, any luck?"

"We're being held by something, and we're not in normal space, either."

"What? I thought the alien ship went to translight after it grabbed us."

"It felt like that, sir, but we didn't decelerate—instead we somehow accelerated to a higher form of hyperspace."

Thom shook his head, incredulous. "Bosun, send a marine squad outside to search the area."

"Yes, sir."

Commander Kennedy was standing before a frontier mansion, with two suns blazing in the sky. He looked around, disoriented.

"Welcome to Alpha Centauri, Commander," said a young woman from the porch. Her hair was long and dark; she wore a purple colonial dress. "I am Hadara. My father is away."

This was familiar to Kennedy, allowing him to dismiss his momentary confusion.

"Hello, miss," he said, trying to maintain the

proper decorum. "I had an appointment to meet the governor—I'm surprised he is not here."

"He should be back shortly. Please come wait inside," she said with an inviting smile.

Kennedy followed her into the front parlor.

"Hey, what gives?" said Cook, the youngest crewman, as he watched the new scene unfolding on the main screen. "Looks like Miss Hadara's here!"

"Stranger than that, Earl" said Thom. "It looks like the captain's at Alpha C colony. This must be a recording of some kind."

Rachel caught her breath at the sight of her fiancé alone with a beautiful woman.

Is this jealousy? she wondered as her stomach knotted up and her fingernails dug into her palms. She whirled on Thom.

"Lieutenant Harris once told me that the captain was a wolf in seven star systems," said Rachel. "Is that an accurate statement?"

Thom laughed uneasily. "Well . . . no. Harris was exaggerating."

"Then how do you explain this?" said Rachel, as on the viewer they saw Hadara throw herself into the captain's arms.

Earl whistled. "Whoa, *captain!*" Then he gave a guilty glance at Rachel. "I mean, "*Whoa,* captain, *whoa!*"

"Please rescue me!" said Hadara, her green eyes boring into his.

"I . . . you . . . what are you doing?" said Kennedy, holding her at arm's length. His confusion was back, redoubled.

"I've loved you since first sight," said Hadara. "Save me from my father. He beats me, and I think he killed my mother—no, I *know* he did. But now I can claim asylum on your ship."

She kissed him hungrily. He tried to hold her away. This was not familiar to Kennedy, but it was not entirely alien, either.

"What in blazes?" said the Governor.

The couple separated.

"Sir, I can explain," said Kennedy, but the enraged older man grappled with him. "It's not what you think—"

The Governor gave a gasp and spun around, a dagger protruding from his back. He sank to the floor.

"What have you done?" said Kennedy, kneeling to help the mortally wounded man.

"He would have killed you," said Hadara.

Kennedy drew the multiphone from his belt. "Kennedy to cruiser, come in."

"It isn't too late," said Hadara. "Take me away!"

"Thom here, captain."

"Send Doc out to the governor's mansion on the double," said Kennedy. "I've got a stabbing victim on hand." He pointed the multiphone's camera at the prone form, thinking, *No, this isn't right…*

"That didn't happen," said Thom, shaking his head. "I was on watch when the captain visited the governor, but I never got a call about a stabbing. And the governor saw us off when we left the planet."

"Squad One to cruiser, over," crackled a voice on the radio speaker.

"Thom here. Go ahead, Squad One."

"Sir, the walls seem to be made of Forerunner metal, but there's nothing flat—it's like we're in a bubble cave. No sign of any doors, sir."

"Any luck finding whatever is holding the ship down?"

"No sir, but we don't really know what we're looking for."

"I'm going out there, too," said Rachel. "With my robot. Give me a space suit."

"I can't allow that," said Thom.

"I love him!"

"You don't know what love is," said Thom with a thinly disguised sneer.

Her blue eyes blazed. "Rob, codeword *Damo*—" she brought herself short.

Thom looked at her, surprised to see her as anything but kittenish.

Her expression softened.

"You can't stop me, Roger," she said, adopting a conciliatory tone. "Wouldn't you go through hell for your fiancée? Besides, I know Forerunner technology—I grew up around it—and that might help."

"I'll send a squad with you," said Thom, seeing her in a new light. "Cook, get her a suit."

"Yes sir!"

"Bosun, form an escort for Rachel," said Thom.

"Yes sir."

"Welcome, captain," said the barmaid. "What'll you have?"

Kennedy glanced around in confusion and saw he was in a crowded log-cabin style saloon, adorned here and there with dinosaur-head hunting trophies. The place was familiar.

I must have been dazzled coming in from the bright outdoors, he thought.

"I'll have a beer," said Kennedy.

"Coming right up," she said. Her dark hair was in a long braid.

The clientele was a rough crowd of miners, ranchers, and lumberjacks. Kennedy had no doubt that many of them had been soldiers on the losing side of the war. Through the window he could see the seething jungle of Epsilon Eridani II.

"Here you go," she said, setting the foaming mug before him. "I'm Erin and this's my place." Her eyes were green.

"I'm Les Kennedy. Cheers." He took a sip of the pungent beer, and then looked around again. "This place is built like a fort."

"My father made it," said Erin. "And he built it to last."

"I have reports of smuggling," Kennedy said quietly. "Do you know anything about that?"

"I couldn't really say," Erin answered, her face hardened into a mask of indifference.

"Is your father around?" he said.

"I don't know," said Erin. "I doubt it." Her cool demeanor suddenly broke and she cried "Papa!" Then she threw herself down behind the counter.

A shot rang out from the doorway and a lead slug splintered the counter next to Kennedy. He whirled away, drawing his sidearm as the bearded man fired two more times, this time winging Kennedy in the left arm and toppling a miner who was running for cover.

Grimacing at the pain, Kennedy squeezed off a shot, sending a high-explosive round into the attacker's chest. The man fell back, a gory corpse.

With a wailing cry, Erin ran to the body.

"Stay back!" said Kennedy to the girl, scanning the crowd that seemed frozen in place.

"This is my father!" she gasped, tears running down her face. "I couldn't tell you, I didn't think he would shoot."

"He was a smuggler, then?" he asked her quietly as he knelt beside her.

"Yes, a bandit chief," she said in a low voice. She choked back a sob. Kennedy put his arm around her, still keeping an eye on the others. She put her face along his shoulder and spoke so nobody else could hear. "Now there's no place for me here—if you don't take me when you go they will kill me." She bit her lip and looked around. "Listen, there are diamonds in the cellar, there must be a pound, you can have them, just take me back to Earth."

"A pound of diamonds?" said Kennedy, licking his lips. He shook himself. "No, no, we'll turn it over to the governor, let him sort it all out." He activated his multiphone. "Kennedy to cruiser, come in."

"Ritchie here, captain."

Kennedy, distracted by the sudden quiet, turned to see that Erin had stopped crying. Her form seemed to be shifting, and for a second she looked like Hadara of the Alpha Centauri colony.

Erin was a colonist, her father was back on Earth, thought Kennedy. *The investigation of smuggling went nowhere. There was no barroom shoot-out.*

"Ritchie here, captain. Come in."

"You aren't the real barmaid," said Kennedy.

"Please repeat, captain?"

"But I am human," she said with a small smile. "A distant cousin."

"Next witness," said the multiphone.

"This looks promising," said space-suited Rachel, pointing to a pocked wall. "It's Forerunner writing."

"It is?" said the bosun.

"Can you read it, Rob?"

"Yes, Miss," said the robot. "It is the emergency release for the anchoring device."

"That's what I thought," said Rachel. "And over here is the airlock." She walked over to another section of the wall where she pushed at some knobby imperfections. A doorway opened.

Rachel smiled as she walked back to the emergency release. She ran her hands over the surface.

"There, the cruiser is now free," she said to the bosun. "You can escape if you like." She walked to the airlock. "Come, Rob."

"Wait!" said the bosun. "You can't go in there!"

"Rob, codeword *Damocles!*"

The bosun tried to grab her but Rachel sprinted away behind the robot, which caught him by the arm.

"Robot, I know you can't kill me," growled the bosun. "You even try it and you'll get a seizure."

"I can break your arm," said Rob conversationally as Rachel went into the airlock. "Or both your legs."

"Easy men," said the bosun to the marines while Rob dragged him into the airlock. "Rachel, please—let us take you back to Earth."

"Thank you, George, but no," said Rachel. "I have to rescue the captain. Or die trying. Push him out, Rob."

Rob shoved the bosun out and closed the airlock.

Rachel and her robot found a dark corridor stretching off into the distance, lit at intervals by glowing ceiling disks. Rob reported a breathable atmosphere, so Rachel took off her helmet and carried it under her arm.

They walked for some minutes before seeing three figures far ahead, at which point they hurried to meet the three judges.

"Hello star traveling beings," said Rachel.

"Greetings, metallic life form," said the mechanical judge to Rob. "You are obviously acquainted with the Forerunners."

"Salutations, fellow robot," said Rob. "I have some degree of literacy for their written words, but little experience with the spoken form."

"This creature is your pet or your servant?" asked the judge.

"*Pet?*" said Rachel, dumbfounded.

"To the contrary," said Rob. "*I* serve *her.*"

There was a moment of awkward silence as the judges looked to each other. Rachel smiled proudly and stood a little taller.

"What is the reason for this servitude?" asked the plantman.

"Her father created me."

"Ah, so she is your stepsister?" asked the judge.

"Wha-*what*?" said Rachel.

"An interesting line of thought, which I have not previously pursued," said Rob. "I suppose 'half-sister' would be more accurate."

"Rob!" said Rachel. "What are you saying?" She held up her hand to halt any answer, shaking her head, with the other hand at her temple. "No, never mind."

She turned to the three.

"Judges, take me to the captain."

For the first time the three judges looked at her. The gray humanoid said, "Yes, that would be best. This way, please."

He led her down a new corridor to the left.

"Come, Rob," she said over her shoulder.

"Our interview with your servant will continue," said the gray humanoid. "It cannot accompany you at this time."

"But . . ."

The judge stopped. "Will you turn back now?"

"No."

"Very well."

They resumed walking. Suddenly they were on a hilltop studded with metal towers having huge propellers spinning in the wind, but the nearest one was still. In the desert valley below stood a city, wondrous to her, and beside the city was a spaceport where she could make out the saucershape of the space cruiser.

"Where are we?" she said, as the breeze pushed

at the soft curls of her shoulder-length hair.

"These are the hills above Mojave, his home-town," said the judge. "Down there is the space-port where you landed. You met his parents, who are now your parents, too. Your long honeymoon is ending, here at this picnic in the shadow of a silent wind turbine."

She noticed she was wearing denim pants, leather boots, and a cowgirl blouse.

"Still getting used to it?" said Kennedy, hugging her from behind.

"The city?"

"The clothes," said Kennedy. He, too, was wearing casual rustic clothing.

"I'll admit I'm not used to wearing pants."

"It's just for hiking, horseback riding, outdoor things like that," said Kennedy. His smile became troubled. "You can wear your dresses when you want."

"No, I probably shouldn't," said Rachel. "What you said back at Altair is true. I must learn modesty and propriety."

"Look at us, getting blue over something so trivial!" said Kennedy. He tried to kiss her but she turned away.

"No, I'm worried," Rachel said. She held her arms, taking a few steps away. "I'm scared. You are going out on that ship again, and it will be months, maybe years, before I see you."

"Honey, haven't we been through all this?" he said. "It's just for a few years, then I'll get that desk job and we'll be set."

"I'll be all alone in a strange new world!"

"My folks are here," he said. "You won't be alone."

"I didn't marry them. I married you."

"You'll be teaching courses on Forerunner science at the university, I'm sure," he said. "Your job will be much more important to the world than mine is, and you will be so busy the time will just fly by."

"I don't like it," she said. "You could die out there."

"Sweetheart . . . "

"It will break my heart if you go," she said. "Sometimes I wish you had never come to Altair. I never knew I was in a prison until you rescued me, but now you are putting me in another one."

"You want me to resign my commission," he said flatly. "Give up the cruiser, everything."

"Yes." She looked up at him with her big blue eyes. Her mouth was compressed into a small red bud.

"We'll have nothing," he said, looking away.

"No, we won't have *nothing*," she said. "We'll have each other. We'll have everything."

"This . . . this is not happening," he said, looking around wildly. "It's another illusion. We're not really on Earth, we're still on the alien ship, and you're that other woman, not really Rachel."

"I *am* Rachel," she said.

"Prove it," he said.

"How can I prove it if they can read your thoughts?"

"Try to tell me something I don't know," said Kennedy.

"You think they don't lie, that they don't bend the truth?" she said. "Did you really fight with the governor of Alpha C?"

"No," he said. "But how did you know about that?"

"They beamed it to the ship," she said. "We watched it like a movie. But listen, Les, did the real barmaid at Epsilon Eridani offer you diamonds?"

"No."

"Then what could I say that wouldn't be something like that?"

"I don't know," he said. "But it wouldn't be something that put me into an ethical dilemma, since that is what the judges do." She was silent, thinking hard. He swept his hand toward the panorama around them. "You're right, this illusion is a complete fantasy since it is not based on an event in the past. It is just a made-up future."

"I wonder about that robot judge," said Rachel. "I mean, we don't really know what the Forerunners looked like, but there were some hints in that 'Caliban' monster . . . "

She shivered once at the memory of Caliban, the implacable ogre-guardian of the Forerunner library. It had killed so many people, ending with her father. Kennedy put his arm around her shoulders.

"So the judge might be a Forerunner robot?"

"Yes, and it would look like them the way that Rob looks human."

"The heir of a vanished species, if it is true."

"Here's something, Les," she said softly. "My robot—the robot ... Rob thinks of itself as my half-brother."

"What?" said Kennedy. "But it's a machine!"

"Built by my father, using Forerunner science." She sighed. "I guess I've always taken it for granted. It is a person, too."

"I hadn't thought of it that way."

"Slavery is bad," she said. "There's an ethical dilemma, but it's mine, not yours."

"Maybe it was set free when your father ... died," said Kennedy. "It serves you now out of duty, but it will not allow itself to be bought or sold."

"Maybe you're right," she said. "We'll have to ask it."

"My problem is this whole Mojave scenario," said Kennedy.

"No, it is just an illusion," said Rachel. "But the sad truth is that our wedding is a marriage of necessity."

"Why 'sad'?" He saw he had said the wrong thing since tears welled up in her eyes.

"I chose you because I love you, but you proposed to me only to protect your ship."

"But I *do* love you!" said Kennedy.

"If I'd chosen Thom or Ritchie, would you have performed the marriage?" she asked, her chin coming up defiantly.

He swallowed, and said, "Yes."

"There it is," said Rachel.

"You had to be married, to protect both you *and* the ship," said Kennedy.

"And when we really get there, I'll let you go back to the ship," said Rachel. "I lost my father, my home world, all just yesterday, and I'm afraid." She wiped the tears away with the back of her hand. "But this is life for all wives of spacemen, so I will accept it. We've already had that fight now, and you won."

"I don't know," he said, hugging her. "I think I will resign, after all."

She stiffened in his arms. "Look!"

The colors of the landscape were shifting, bleeding away. The gold of the dry grass, the green of the valley farms, all running up. The blue sky itself was last, revealing it was just a fuzzy ceiling, and where the city had stood in the distance was now a blank wall only 100 yards away. The dry grass of the hill became silver, as did the stump of the nearest wind turbine, and all began to melt into the ground, which flattened into a floor.

"My clothes!" said Rachel as her cowgirl outfit dissolved to reveal the spacesuit beneath.

Kennedy was in his uniform again.

A door opened, admitting the three judges, Rob, and the brunette woman. The woman carried

Rachel's space helmet, which she handed to her.

"The trial is over," said the humanoid. "We find Commander Kennedy not guilty of planetary destruction. We find Commander Kennedy not guilty of scientific theft."

"You understand, now, that Rachel's father destroyed the planet?" said Kennedy.

"Yes, and he was the one with the most knowledge of the Forerunners," said the humanoid. "His death, while unfortunate, saves us the dilemma of his knowledge spreading to Earth."

"But a new complication arose in the form of Rob and Rachel," said the plant-man. "Both possess a lesser degree of Forerunner knowledge, and while they are not thieves, still there is a problem . . ."

"We find humankind to be a primitive race," said the alien robot. "Such little Forerunner knowledge as these two have could cause serious trouble for humanity as well as the interstellar community. Yet death is too harsh a sentence, so we will release you all, and your starship."

"What kind of beings are you, that you assume such godlike powers?" asked Rachel.

"We are far below the Forerunners," said the plant-man, "but still high above you."

"Captain," said the humanoid. "If you see a neighbor's farmhouse burn down, and you witness a group of youngsters running away, are you not obligated to stop them and question them as to the circumstances?"

After a moment of consideration, Kennedy said, "I see your point. But tell me, did you know the Forerunners?"

"When we were like you are, they stood to us as we stand to you today," said the humanoid. "Even though they have been gone some millions of years, still we remember them well and serve to honor their memory."

"Who is she?" Rachel asked the robotic judge. "I thought she was pure illusion."

"She is Maghu, a justice dancer," said the judge. "Her ancestors were specimens collected from Earth less than a million years ago."

"It was my honor and pleasure to serve you as prosecutor and defender," Maghu said to Kennedy. She gave an elaborate bow.

"Is she your *pet*?" said Rachel.

"Naturally," said the alien robot. "But in the cluster her kind occupy a dozen worlds or more . . ."

" . . . so by the powers invested in me by space law," said the bosun, "I hereby pronounce you husband and wife."

The men cheered as the couple kissed, completing their wedding in warpspace.

"Thank you, everyone," said Kennedy. "Now all hands to trans-light stations! Less than a minute until the judges toss us free."

Rachel stood on the pad near the captain's. The transparent tubes descended from the ceiling and protected each person with a forcefield for the transition between energy states.

The transit from warpspace to hyperspace was violent but not deadly. It lasted a few minutes, and then the captain's tube retracted. Rachel saw him leave his pad and walk over to the helm. After some adjustments, he came back to his pad. The tube lowered over him and the ship made the transition from hyperspace to normal space.

All the tubes went up and the men went to their stations.

"Let's see where we are," said Thom.

"Can't be too far off," said Kennedy. "Even if warpspace is a hundred times faster than hyperspace, we were only there for an hour."

"Captain, I'm not recognizing anything."

"Rob, give us a hand here, please," said Kennedy. "Locate Altair."

After a few seconds the robot indicated a faint star.

"But captain," said Thom. "That star's magnitude is way off—it must be hundreds of light years away!"

"Assume Rob is right and check the bright stars around us," said Kennedy. "Any patterns emerge?"

"A lot of blue stars, ten of them," said Thom. "Four of them are giants . . . no, it can't be!"

"What is it?"

"Captain, we're in the Pleiades!"

"Impossible! Let me look at that. Rob, come take a look. Is this the Pleiades cluster?"

The robot studied for a moment. "Yes. There is Alcyone, Atlas, and Pleione."

"Captain, we must be 400 light years from Earth!"

"That's 25 years of travel at our best speed!"

"The judges said that the trial was over," said Kennedy, "but maybe a new one is beginning."

"Oh no," said Rachel, stepping close to Kennedy. He dropped a protective arm across her shoulders. "This must be our sentence—exile from Earth."

"Is this a new test, Rob?" asked Kennedy. "Do the judges want to see if we destroy ourselves with Forerunner technology, or if we have the maturity to master it?"

"It seems quite likely, sir."

"Captain, I'm picking up hyperwave signals from a few of the nearby star systems."

"Let's hear it," said Kennedy, giving his wife a hug. "Maybe someone will give us a warpspace drive as a wedding present."

MY FOUR FOUNDLING FATHERS

The family is an invention that, like all inventions, has gone through periods of use and abandonment. When the Restoration came to America in the twenty-first century, the family was re-introduced as a socio-economic and political unit. But even in its second decade the Restoration was fragile, and vigilance was required. The new Minutemen were not soldiers. They were watchers.

Two Internet Content Officers, Mrs. Sally Williams and Mrs. Veronica Salt, began their shift at the police center, patrolling the data stream within their Altifornian district. Tension was higher than normal that Friday night due to the sudden imposition of a curfew. With access denied to the ice cream parlors, opera houses, and community theaters, the Internet traffic would be heavier than usual.

The officers did not wear uniforms—Sally was

in a granny dress and Veronica had on a work shirt and blue jeans—but both were grandmothers in their forties, with the legal minimum number of grandchildren. For Sally that was eight; Veronica, a lesbian, had twelve. Their workstations were side by side, and they skimmed new programming as it appeared.

Sally, watching a video, sputtered her coffee in mid-sip.

"Hey, I think I've got something."

"You recording yet?" asked Veronica, scooting her office chair over.

"I am now." Sally restarted the video and said, "Watch this."

"Hello, I'm . . . somebody," said the man on the screen. He was in his late twenties, sitting in a bare white room and talking straight at the camera. "I'm a survivor. In the bad old days I was a 'toy,' a kind of living prop used in a so-dram—a social drama."

Sally paused the video. "See, he actually said it. That's counter-Restoration."

"Is it still on the list of forbidden terms? I think it's in a gray zone now."

"Things have become lax," said Sally, nodding at the empty workstations around them.

"Hmm, it's labeled 'Educational, PG-13,'" said Veronica.

They frowned and pondered. The man was obviously not in a classroom, and he wasn't dressed like a teacher.

"We should watch more and see," said Veronica.

Sally started the video. The man said, "If you're old enough, you might remember me from such so-drams as . . . no, no names. All of that is over now."

Sally paused it. "You recognize him?"

Veronica shook her head.

"Me neither. Maybe it's a sham."

She started it again.

The man leaned forward, conspiratorially, so his face filled the screen, and said in a soft voice, "This is my show. I call it 'My Four Foundling Fathers,' but that's our secret for now."

He resumed his previous posture and voice. "I'm sitting in the 'Green Room,' which is behind the scenes—in the past it would be the one vidcam-free room in a given location. So this isn't one hundred percent historically accurate, but my purpose is to show the old, forbidden art from both the 'stage' and the 'backstage,' to borrow those terms from theater. This is also a free-view room, at least for now. Anyway, this is where we talk naturally."

A small-framed, pixie-like woman entered from stage right to stand behind him, saying, "*If you look in this place tomorrow, and it's gone, you mustn't be sad, because you know it still exists, not very far away.*"

It was Audrey Infree, and Sally was thirteen again, watching her in a so-dram when Sally's stepsister came in crying that her stepdad had died of an overdose. She was twenty-one again, watching Audrey in a different so-dram when Sally's phone rang, from her mother's boyfriend, with the news that her half-brother had been killed by a rival gang. She was thirty again, watching Audrey in a so-dram in an attempt to push the abortion out of her mind. The actress had been one she identified with, one who had been there with her at terrible points in her life.

Veronica reached over and paused it. "Whoa, he's not faking it."

"Yeah. You recognize her? Wow, what a lucky adoption for whoever got her."

"But what would she be? She's in her forties, at least, so she'd be a 'quirky grandma' or a 'widowed aunt' type."

"Yeah," said Sally, nodding with enthusiasm. "'Auntie.' But why is she doing this? She is shaming her family."

"Maybe he will just interview her. Let's find out."

She started it again.

"What?" said the man, half turning to see the pixie-woman.

"I thought you started."

"This is the Green Room."

"So why's that here, then?" she asked, pointing at the vidcam and the viewers beyond it.

"Everyone," he said, turning back to the camera, "this is Audrey.'"

"Well, backstage, maybe," she said, making a face. "But what about out there?"

"Audrey. The same."

"So who are you, now?"

"I'm Star."

"Oh, ha-ha," she giggled. "Okay."

Turning to the watchers again, Star said, "Audrey had a variety of roles. In one so-dram I was her little brother, in another one I was her nephew. Never was her son, I don't think."

"No, I never had a mom-job. I'm just not the type."

Sally paused it.

"Wait a sec, he isn't *sure?*"

"Yeah," said Veronica. "Because, you know . . . before he was a little kid with memories, he was a baby without memories."

"Ugh."

Sally restarted it.

"Wow," said Star, "talking like this really takes me back! Has it already been *ten years* since the Restoration?"

"No, it's been twelve."

"You're right! Some of our viewers might be so young they don't really remember."

"Say, what's your rating for this?" said Audrey.

"PG-13. I thought this was going for the nostalgia market, but yeah, it's also educational, too."

"It was an art form," she said with a sniff.

"Okay, so it's our first day on a new so-dram—let's recreate for them what that was like."

"The first step was handing out the identikits," said Audrey. "Speaking of which, Star-darling, how are we going to do that?"

"Everyone, she's talking about the role-cards and fake photos that would define each person and their relationship to each other, for the duration of the so-dram. Right? So we'd get this shoebox full of stuff, like maybe a scuffed up baseball, and some old war medals, and always photographs. Things that might or might not be used for set dressing later, but were sort of like talismans. They were emotional touchstones for the characters we were to become."

"You always seemed to be pretty intense about that," said Audrey.

"How do you mean?"

"Staring at the photos, making up little stories, stuff like that."

"That's true," said Star. "What was it like for you, on the first day of a new thing?"

"Well, I'd look over the stuff, of course, but on the first day?" She struck a thoughtful pose, with hand on chin. "I'd be wondering how long it would last, hoping that it would be a long one. Of course things can get *too* long, but that's a problem I'd like to have, because getting a bunch of short things is pretty rough."

"Yeah, and that's my whole life in so-drams," said Star. "Or was. A couple or three five-year deals, and a whole bunch of one or two year deals."

"Five years is pretty good."

"Where does 'long' start?"

"Seven or eight, I guess," said Audrey with a slight shrug.

Sally paused it.

"Well, I—I never knew that," she said. "I watched plenty of those things, like everybody else did, but I never thought about how they were made."

"That's what was so sick about them, and the times," said Veronica. "They were pretending. Their lives were a lie, with no line between fiction and real. That sort of decadence could only be repaired by the Restoration."

"This certainly seems to be 'educational' so far. Hey, that line she used before, do you recognize it?"

"Sure. It's a rare one, but the way she said it really sent me back! She was always a good one, even when she was being naughty."

Sally clicked on play, and Audrey continued talking.

"But anyway, how are we going to do the identikit part? We don't have crew to set that up."

"I'll do it," said Star.

"*You?*"

"Yes. You're my aunt Audrey. Sister to my mother."

"Younger sister?"

"Of course!"

"I'll take it."

A seedy rogue burst in from stage right. "*You*

can't handle the truth!" he said, a maniacal grin upon his face.

Sally felt a visceral shock at the sight of this actor. Jack Mickelsson represented the worst side of men—he was selfish, treacherous, lecherous, predatory, and sinister. He was like her father, her stepdad, and most of her mother's boyfriends.

Veronica hit the pause and said, "Wow, it's him!"

Sally, who had been thinking that a few years of hard labor at a community garden would help Jack in his re-education, instead said, "I would've thought he left the country."

"Plenty would adopt him."

"But would he allow himself to be adopted?" asked Sally. "I don't think so."

"He'd have to be a bachelor uncle, I'll grant you that."

Veronica restarted the video.

"Relax," said Audrey to the newcomer, "it's the Green Room."

His brow knitted with real irritation, he pointed into the screen and said, "Well then how come—"

"Hush, he's handing out identikits."

"Hello, Jack," said Star. "Dad."

"'Jack'?" he said, shaking his head as if dazed. "'Dad'?"

(The officers agreed with him, snorting their disbelief.)

"There you go," said Audrey. "Work with it."

"And what, you're 'Mom'?" asked Jack. "*I never mean to hurt you, and yet it's all I ever do.*"

"No, I'm sister to Mom," she said. "And save your lines—they're all wasted here."

"Jack, she's Audrey."

"Hmmm. I'm *dying* of suspense—let's get this moving, huh? I'll just send the rest of them in." He exited, stage right.

"One at a time, please," said Star.

From off-screen came the sound of a door opening, followed by Jack's voice calling out, "Hey *Mom*, you're up!"

After a while, a former beauty queen entered, stage right.

Sally gasped at the rush of conflicting emotions unleashed upon seeing Venus Hayworth. She had been a guilty pleasure—Sally had secretly wanted to be such a powerful woman, using her beauty to get her way with men, but now the actress was emblematic of the pre-Restoration chaos.

"'Mom'?" said Venus, stiffly regal in her fifties.

Sally hit the pause, saying, "Oh, that's wrong. Look at her hair—too long, and that fake color!"

"Does she think she is still a school girl? Hussy!"

"The Lifestyle Police would punish her on the spot," said Sally, wanting to see such a thing.

"I'm pretty sure she left the country," said Veronica. "Who would adopt her, anyway? She embodies the worst of it."

"Well, the fact that she looks like that proves she wasn't adopted, that's for sure," said Sally before starting it again.

"Yes, that's right," said Star. "I name you Venus."

A man wearing glasses walked in from stage right, his fingers nervously twiddling the patch of hair on the top of his head. Sally smiled at seeing this one. Woody Cohen had been a jokester. He showed a disturbing side in his later so-drams, but even then he was fairly wholesome compared to Jack Micklesson.

"I've been thinking," he said. "Maybe I could be the butler or the chef? I don't want to step on your plans, but—"

"Hello, Woody. Dad."

"Whoa! I thought you gave that to—well hey, what kind of deal is this, anyway? Are we a gay couple, me and him? No offense, but I'd prefer either of these ladies."

A debonair man with silver hair walked in from stage right and stopped, waiting just inside the frame. Sally rested her jaw on her palm and sighed looking at Cary Granite. He was the dreamboat, the good-looking nice man. As a child, Sally always wanted her mother to find a boyfriend like him, and as a woman she had tried to find one for herself.

Star said, "Ladies and gentleman, this is Cary. Hello, Dad."

"Well, that makes two—"

"It's up to three now," said Venus, putting her hand on her ample hip and smiling archly.

"Ah," said Cary, moving in to stand behind Star. "Perhaps this is some weird, experimental commune? Actually, that could be pretty interesting."

From stage right, a grizzled old cowboy stumped into the room. Sally gave a puzzled smile for this one—he was a good guy, hardworking.

"Well, here I am," said Ron Wayne, striking at his barrel chest. "What ya got for me?"

"Hello, Ron. Dad."

"Well now, huh."

"So is this a group marriage, or serial monogamy?" asked Cary.

"Polyandrous?" said Audrey.

"It sure ain't Pollyanna, I can tell you that," said Ron, hitching up his belt.

"You may be wondering why I gathered you here today," said Jack with a sneering grin as he entered the picture again.

"My four foundling fathers," said Star. "We will now leave the Green Room—"

"What, that's *it*?" roared Ron Wayne.

Woody stepped forward and leaned around Star to speak directly at the vidcam, his face filling the screen. "*Also in this house dwells Pseudolus, slave to his son. Pseudolus is probably my favorite character in the piece, a role of enormous variety and nuance, and played by an actor of such versatility, such magnificent . . . Let me put it this way. I play the part.*"

"Gentlemen," said Star, pulling Woody back,

"follow me to the living room. Ladies, go to the kitchen and prepare a meal."

"But what's the scene?" demanded Jack.

Star, heading stage right, said, "It's like Thanksgiving, with us hanging out, waiting for a big meal."

On the screen popped up a button marked "Hallway (free view)."

"Do we agree that the 'mother' is a paperless?" asked Veronica.

"Yes. Definitely below homeless."

"What if . . . they are *all* paperless?"

"Most of them seem quite adoptable to me, but it would make sense, I guess."

"Where did he find all these pariahs?" asked Veronica. "How big is this thing?"

"On the bright side, if it turns out to be criminal, they are all in one place."

"You recognize the others?"

"A little," said Sally. "Especially the suave guy. I always liked him."

"I had a thing for 'Jack,' myself."

Sally looked at Veronica with new eyes. She had always assumed that Veronica was one of the rare few to have had a family as a child, but now she wondered if Veronica's early life had been like her own.

Pushing these thoughts aside, Sally asked, "Where is this heading? Do they want another Amnesty?"

"If he just interviews them, that might be

okay."

Sally activated the hallway button. The following scene had a strange point of view, from above, like a fly's view from the corner. Star went upstage a bit, then through a door stage right, followed by Jack, Ron Wayne, and Cary Granite. The women went straight upstage to another door. Woody was last, and after a funny bit of back and forth hesitation, he sneaked away to follow the women. Two buttons appeared.

"Well, we've crossed a line," said Sally, referring to the camera work. "Maybe we should file a report and quit?"

"Kitchen or living room?" asked Veronica.

Sally sighed. "Living room."

She hit the button for the living room and they got a payment page. There was a price to watch, but there were also "tips" buttons for paying each of the participants.

"Now what?" asked Sally. "Can't use the department card on this, and I'd rather not have my name associated with something so questionable."

"So use an anonymous card. What, you don't have one? Here, I'll do it. You owe me half."

The clip started with the men just figuring out that Woody had slipped away, but they let it go with shrugs and snorts. Cary Granite stood by the fireplace as the others sat down in upholstered chairs. It looked like a real house, so the men were facing toward the fireplace, like the audience of a play within a play, but then there was a viewpoint shift, centered on Jack, who said, "I'll bet you-know-who is talking about a morning meal at the jewelry store."

The officers grinned at that, exchanging glances.

Veronica paused it to say, "This vidcam work, the shifting, is like being on a rollercoaster."

"Yeah, or being in a funhouse barrel. I had forgotten that."

"But it comes back, like riding a bicycle," said Veronica, before starting it again.

"*Well, art is art, isn't it?*" said Cary. "*Still, on the other hand, water is water. And east is east and west is west, and if you take cranberries and stew them like applesauce, they taste much more like prunes than rhubarb does. Now, uh . . . Now you tell me what you know.*"

Ron Wayne turned and addressed the others with, "*I'm telling you: Who's on first, What's on second, I Don't Know is on third.*"

The officers groaned and laughed. Sally paused it.

"It's funny that he used that old line, but I don't get it."

"The first guy is commenting on the artless 'art' they are practicing," said Veronica. "The next guy is trying to figure out the pecking order of the men regarding the hussy."

Veronica clicked on the tips button for Ron Wayne.

"Say, Veronica," said Sally. "Did you—? This is really personal, and you don't have to answer, but . . . did you have a family, a real family, before the Restoration?"

"No," said Veronica, and Sally felt a burst of kinship with her, a rush of validation. But then Veronica blushed beet-red and stammered, "Yes, I did, but I—I covered it up."

"You *what?*" cried Sally, her warm and fuzzy feeling snatched away.

"I wanted to be like everybody else," said Veronica, talking to the fists in her lap. "I was ashamed. And frightened."

Sally fought against dark feelings of outrage and betrayal. She said, "You poor thing," and having said the reflexive platitude, she actually began to feel genuine sympathy.

Sally started the video again.

"*I'm sick of these conventional marriages,*" said Cary. "*One woman and one man was good enough for your grandmother, but who wants to marry your grandmother? Nobody, not even your grandfather.*"

Veronica paused it.

"See, now that's a line supporting the Restoration. Bravo!"

She clicked a tip for Cary Granite, then restarted the video.

Jack turned to Star. "*If your daddy really did come back, could you make believe that . . . look, could you pretend that . . . that he'd never been away?*"

The room was quiet for a moment, as if some

gaffe had been committed, or a challenge had been given.

(The officers leaned forward, alert.)

Star said, "*I don't know if you'd be particularly interested in hearing anything about me. My life, I mean ... Most of it doesn't add up to much that I could relate as a way of life.*"

A quick sequence of close-ups revealed that the older men were stunned.

(Both officers were speechless, with their mouths hanging open.)

"*By George, I think he's got it,*" said Ron Wayne. He and Cary looked impressed, as if Star had really done something, but Jack looked angry.

The point of view changed so Jack sat stage-right and Star sat stage-left.

"*I'm sorry it didn't work out,*" said Star to Jack, which only seemed to make him worse.

"*Son, we live in a world that has walls, and those walls are ...*" Jack paused to look around conspiratorially, "full of eyes and ears."

From the next room came a scream, a heavy thump, and a cry for help. The men rushed out of the room, ending the clip.

The officers burst into talk.

"Did you see—"

"How could he—"

"That was really like it!"

"But he's so young," said Sally. "How could he use a line like that?"

"Yeah, using one of Jack's famous lines against

him! Incredible!"

"But how?"

"He grew up among those types," said Veronica. "He must've heard it all, a lot more than we ever did."

"I guess. Either that or it is scripted, and that would be cheating."

Sally clicked back to the hallway, then clicked "Previous Scene" in order to get the kitchen button.

"We have to see what happened before the scream," she said, "so we'll pay for the full clip rather than just when the men come in. If that's all right with you?"

"Yes," said Veronica.

The price for the kitchen-view was pretty high, but the officers were hooked now, so Veronica paid it.

At first the viewpoint was as if from a fly in the corner of the ceiling, but then it went black and brightened suddenly as if from a mouse inside the cabinet when Woody opened the cabinet door. Then it went black and brightened with a view from inside the refrigerator when Audrey opened that door.

Toward the end, it settled down and almost became like a cooking show.

Woody said, "*Now, an egg is not a stone. It is not made of wood. It is a living thing. It has a heart. So when we crack it we must not torment it. We must be merciful and execute it quickly, like with a guillotine.*"

"*Babette knows how to cook,*" said Audrey.

"*It's amazing what you can do with a cheap piece of meat if you know how to treat it,*" said Woody.

"*Well, bring the dog,*" said Venus. "*I love animals. I'm a great cook.*"

And then Venus fell over without a word, just a little half-groan. Audrey screamed, Venus landed on her side, rolling partly onto her back, and Woody yelled for help.

The others ran in. Ron Wayne tried to rouse Venus and Cary picked up the receiver from the wall-mounted telephone and called for paramedics.

The video segment ended abruptly.

The officers looked at each other in mute surprise.

"Is it real, or is it fake?" asked Veronica.

There was a button for the living room. The price was high. Veronica paid it.

All the people were in the room except for Venus. They were dressed in black and most were seated, the exceptions being Ron Wayne and Cary Granite, who stood on either side of the fireplace.

The view shifted to frame Woody, stage right, and Audrey, stage left.

"*I've seen this before,*" said Woody. "*It happens to old people.*"

"*The stars are ageless,*" said Audrey. "*Aren't they?*"

The viewpoint changed to Star, seen in profile leaning on his knees, saying, "She was in her fifties.

Not that old."

The view went to Cary, his arm resting on the mantelpiece. Looking like a portrait, he said, "*Fifty—the old age of youth, the youth of old age.*"

The view pulled back until framed by Audrey, stage right, and Jack, stage left.

"*I believe I am past my prime,*" said Audrey. "*I had reckoned on my prime lasting till I was at least fifty.*"

"*Death,*" said Jack. "*What do you all know about death?*"

The view continued to pull back, showing all the seated.

"*Life's a city full of straying streets,*" said Audrey, "*and death's the marketplace where each one meets. Just like that.*"

"*But there are times when suddenly you realize you're nearer the end than the beginning,*" said Ron Wayne. "*I don't know whether that kind of thinking's very healthy, but I must admit I've had some thoughts on those lines from time to time.*"

"*Death ends a life,*" said Cary, "*but it does not end a relationship, which struggles on in the survivor's mind toward some resolution which it may never find.*"

The view snapped over to gaze upon Star, who had been staring at the floor and shaking his head at most of the lines, but now he looked up at Cary with shining eyes.

Then the view shifted to a new point, as though seen from the mantle itself. Now the audience was on stage, and the two standing men were the audience.

"*I have a very low threshold of death,*" said Woody. "*And that's all I have to say about that.*"

"*That's the unfortunate thing about death,*" said Audrey. "*It's so terribly final.*"

"*A lot more people are going to die before this is over,*" said Jack.

"Oh, shut up," said Star. "This is not a death march."

"*There are far worse things facing man than death,*" said Cary.

"*This is my life,*" said Audrey. "*It always will be. There's nothing else. Just us and the cameras and those wonderful people out there in the dark.*"

"I wanted . . . " said Star. "Look. The plan I had is ruined. You all need help. Once you were high and celebrated, but now you are low, forgotten, penniless. You six—no, you five, now—have become the forgotten toys, the toys in the attic. The fact that our roles have become reversed is ironic, almost a kind of revenge for me, but I really, honestly wanted to help you by making this kind of household, this family, where you could use your talents.

"But Venus was the hub of the whole thing, and without her here, I can't see the rhyme or reason of the project."

"Perhaps a change in roles?" said Audrey in a quiet voice.

"No, that's the whole point," said Star, "the Mystery of Family. There are no changes, like the shuffles that go on between so-drams—in a family the roles are carved in bone, written in blood. So no, you cannot go from aunt to mother here."

"*I love you, like my son that I'll never see,*" said Ron Wayne.

Star laughed a half-sob. "Yes, right, that's the sort of thing you would be saying many sessions later, weeks or months from now, after our household had gone through various ups and downs. But so early, and in this situation, it seems hollow and meaningless."

"*I sold flowers,*" said Audrey. "*I didn't sell myself. Now you've made a lady of me, I'm not fit to sell anything else.*"

"*I'm sorry it didn't work out,*" said Star, using that line again.

"*Well,*" said Audrey, tenderly, "*what family doesn't have its ups and downs?*"

Star buried his face in his hands and began sobbing. Audrey bent down to whisper something in his ear. She seemed to repeat herself, and then he nodded.

Straightening up, she turned and walked to the camera so her face filled the whole screen. She said, "*If you look in this place tomorrow, and it's gone, you mustn't be sad, because you know it still exists, not very far away.*" And then she reached over and turned it off. Ending the clip.

It was over. There were no new buttons.

Sally and Veronica had tears in their eyes.

Still, Sally flagged the video, Veronica counter-signed, and they submitted the report to their superior, a grandmother with sixteen grandchildren.

"It's for the best," said Sally.

"It's out of our hands," said Veronica. "Who knows, maybe it will pass inspection—"

Just then the video went offline.

"Wow," said Sally. "There's the answer."

"Now I wonder if we're going to get in trouble for being so slow to flag it."

"Well, we did, anyway."

"It was ... like a swansong."

"Maybe it was a test from higher up."

Whether it was a test or not remains unclear, but a purge followed quickly. Veronica Salt was among those privileged urban party members who were arrested and sentenced to open-ended terms of rustification at government farm camps. Their families were dissolved, with each member becoming a ward of the state, usually organized into homeless labor units.

Because the Restoration was fragile, and vigilance was required to protect America from threats domestic as well as foreign.

BELLEROFONTE

In golden Cibola, when a kite pilot falls to his death during the games he is called "Icaro," after the mythic one who flew too close to the Sun. When a flier falls but survives, he is called "Bellerofonte" for the one who never flew again after being thrown by the horse with wings. Usually the games do not involve such disasters since they are all about counting coup, but "accidents" do happen.

On this particular afternoon the slight breeze was coming from the Pacific Ocean to the west, with the ground warm enough to generate thermals, those invisible geysers of uplifting air. In short it was weather perfect for aerial jousting at the Anaheim Mandala, a human hive dominating the orange groves for miles around it.

Participation in the games was voluntary, but viewing was mandatory, with tequila for the elites, mezcal for the respectables, and moonshine for the rest.

The game had roots in the ancient Wind Dancers, where the four winds were ranked and associated with colors. The flying order and starting positions were awarded to each kite pilot by earned ranking: black on top, then yellow, next red, and finally green at the bottom. Always four: no more, no less.

For this particular meet there was a last minute substitution of the green pilot due to food poisoning. This replacement entered the jousting lists as "Bellerofonte." Scraggly long blond hair stuck out from beneath his green helmet, and his nervous smile showed rotten, crooked teeth, while sunglasses hid his eyes. A stereotypical sudden replacement: a loser probably lured out of retirement with the promise of a bottle of mezcal.

Upon the skyscraping heliport, Bellerofonte avoided gazing at the other three pilots by facing east toward the enormous slope of the Anaheim Mandala. Like a giant roof, the rough concrete stretched three thousand feet from north to south and the same vast reach from ridge to eaves. Built when powered flight had been common, the heliport jutted up from the middle of the slope like a titanic chimney.

Bellerofonte turned from this to focus on the mandala's twin over at Santa Ana, seven miles away. From this angle he could see the hive as a square concrete box set on point, supported by squat towers. Within the open-ended box a series of internal terraces created a "god's eye" pattern that gave this form the name "mandala."

In addition to the pilots and their kites on the heliport there were the judges with their binoculars, the cable TV crew piping visuals into the hive, the horn section, and various officials, one of whom signaled to the pilot black. This accomplished flier took up the black hang glider, strode confidently to the edge at four thousand feet above the ground, and launched off. The yellow pilot checked his quiver of barbed sticks before following. The red pilot pushed off in a rush.

Bellerofonte hobbled as he carried the green hang glider to the edge. He fought the sudden queasy fear of falling with a final check of his weaponry, and then launched into the air.

He dropped one level for minimal speed, as if reluctant to follow the other three in their race to find the thermal along the road to the Santa Ana hive.

Yellow signaled he had found a thermal. Bellerofonte dropped a level and closed, then the four maneuvered into forming the starting column. Black went first, riding the fast inner thermal up. Yellow took the slower outer thermal up, while red circled the thermals but kept out. Green Bellerofonte dropped a level to get into position.

Soon the column was complete, with each glider one level apart. They circled outside of the thermals, waiting for the signal.

The great Los Angeles plain stretched out before Bellerofonte, dotted with the Seven Cities of Cibola. The Anaheim Mandala was enormous, three quarters of a mile tall, dwarfing the nearest range of hills and challenging the mountains beyond. To the southeast stood two hives: the Santa

Ana Mandala, with the Irvine Treestump behind it.

The horns sounded a call to the wind god Ehecatl, and the contest began.

Bellerofonte's first task was to gain altitude. He broke from the column to hunt another thermal further along the road. By good luck he immediately hit a small satellite thermal, experiencing the upward tug on the kite. Just as he left the thermal a shadow came from above and he dodged left as hard as he could. He felt the tap as a barbed stick attached to his wing, and heard the rustle as the red streamers unfurled.

"Coup!" shouted red, his attacker.

"Olé!" shouted the crowd from Anaheim Mandala's terraces, the god's-eye acting as a megaphone for a few hundred thousands.

Bellerofonte continued turning left to catch the thermal again, while red's momentum carried him further from it. He could not tell what the other two were doing but it seemed unlikely that they would risk ganging up on him: yellow had probably broken out for another thermal, leaving black at the top. Most likely they figured that Bellerofonte would be grounded early by several easy coup-sticks and then it would settle into a jousting among three thermals, spawned by the road below.

Bellerofonte feigned fear and uncertainty through his movement of the kite. Red closed in for an easy hit. At the last second Bellerofonte twitched his glider to the side, rammed red, and then performed a climbing half-loop. While red was stunned, Bellerofonte dropped on him and ripped his wing with a slash of a barbed stick.

Half the crowd booed at this. The horns declared a foul.

As crippled red began his decent, Bellerofonte returned to hunting the next thermal. Finding it, he rose up, watching the lazy jousting of black and yellow until he climbed far enough above them that the horns blared about his excessive altitude. He leveled off.

Black and yellow were making their preliminary passes at each other. Bellerofonte wondered if they had seen his encounter with red, and he guessed that they had not, since a distraction by the one would be exploited by the other. Probably they thought he had accidentally grounded red through some nervous mistake.

So he had an advantage in surprise.

Unfortunately he had his own problem to solve. The treacherous pilot flying as black was his personal enemy. Entering the fray with black and yellow entailed two choices: side with black to tag the weaker yellow; or work with yellow to overcome the stronger black, and in doing so, open himself to attack from his momentary ally.

Or he could attack first one and then the other, getting them to unite against him.

Otherwise he could linger on high, waiting. This would certainly fit the mode of fear and uncertainty that he had been pretending.

But waiting would only use up whatever surprise he had.

With this resolved, he sped toward the pair.

Yellow saw him coming, so by one calculation Bellerofonte should strike at black with surprise. But this only sharpened Bellerofonte's strategy, and he dove instead at the yellow glider nearly head on.

Yellow slipped to the side in a mild evasion, but as Bellerofonte shot over him he planted a barbed green stick in the wing. Then, knowing that black above was watching, Bellerofonte performed a climbing half-loop. Up and back he flipped his kite, bringing the triangle of the yellow glider beneath his feet.

"Olé!" shouted the crowd.

"Icaro!" cried black, recognizing in the execution of that artful maneuver a deadman's signature.

No doubt he was recalling that the body was never found in that odd case by Long Beach, the same game that had cemented his career.

Using a barbed stick, Bellerofonte ripped the yellow wing with easy efficiency. The crowd roared with outrage, and the horns sounded another foul as yellow began his forced landing.

Bellerofonte peered up through his wing-window as he hand-walked a turn, watching to see how his enemy would react to the unmasking. Black might strike, he might flee. He might even strike while fleeing for the ground, which would be a strong move, but one that would put him in the vulnerable lower position.

Black fled, but he fled upward.

Bellerofonte chuckled and followed. This was his dream coming true: just the two of them, high up, facing off with only their flying skills.

They rose up. The altitude horns blared.

Suddenly black broke from the thermal into a steep dive toward the Anaheim Mandala. Bellerofonte followed, dropping for maximum speed. He gained a bit but then the distance between them locked as they raced.

They shot below the altitude of the heliport. Just as the horns declared "out of bounds," Bellerofonte realized with a shock that his enemy was aiming for the eye of the mandala. Rapidly he calculated that he could fly over the hive and catch black on the other side of the hole, but then he considered that once he had broken off, black might double back or even land within the hole, seeking shelter therein.

Landing would be forfeiture, but clearly the game was over. In more ways than one.

Bellerofonte cursed his slowness in grasping what should have been obvious.

Approaching the eye was like diving into the gaping maw of a monster mountain. Bellerofonte expected that air currents would get very turbulent in the cavernous part of the structure. Each ridge of the iris-like Big Hole would be a little different, and the smooth Pupil airway, should they get that far, would be a wind tunnel.

They flew into the cavernous funnel of the Big Hole, a world of diagonal terrain where staggered condos were arranged like rows of teeth marching up to the gullet of the Pupil. About twelve hundred feet deep, with micro-thermals buffeting them and a swelling stream of air pushing them along.

The amphitheater-shape of the Big Hole magnified the sound of a few hundred thousand people into a surf roar. A chorus of barking dogs rippled through the thunder like chain lightning.

It seemed suicidal to attempt a landing on a balcony. Black's goal must be the Pupil, to touch down or to pass through.

As the fliers flew further, the hanging offices above and the condos below seemed to be closing toward them like the jaws of a cubist shark god. The breeze increased as they approached the Pupil, a diamond-shaped opening around seven hundred feet from corner to corner.

Then they were inside the airway.

The air currents were more capricious near the vast diagonal walls, but his enemy began dropping fast. Bellerofonte was ready, and seeing the strategy of landing in the diamond-shaped tunnel, kept hard on his tail.

The sound of human thunder receded further and further behind them. The quiet was almost deafening.

The lower the fliers dipped, the closer they came to those sandpaper slopes.

The tunnel floor was a narrow road, and the first hatch became apparent to both pilots at the same moment. Black initiated a recklessly rapid descent. His left wing tip touched the rough concrete, the kite pivoted to slam into the slope, and then it tumbled down like a leaf from a tree.

Bellerofonte flew past to land on the road between the crash and the hatch. He got out of his rig, took up a barbed stick, and hurried toward his enemy with a crippled jog.

Black stirred, saw his nemesis approaching, and scrambled with frantic efforts. He was out of the rig and lifting a barbed stick when Bellerofonte jabbed him in the side, drawing blood.

Black thrust, but Bellerofonte blocked it, then made a thrust of his own. His enemy dodged but winced, showing signs of damage he had taken in his crash landing.

Bellerofonte felt confidence at this, but then his enemy said, "Back to Hell, you!"

Bellerofonte botched a parry, allowing his enemy's barbed stick to prick his leg. His good leg.

Furious, Bellerofonte unleashed a flurry of jabs and slashes that his enemy grimly blocked or parried.

But the man was weakening through loss of blood from his wound and the trauma of his crash. When he stumbled, Bellerofonte skewered him in the guts, then yanked the other barbed stick from black's fading grasp.

The dying man laughed weakly and said, "I did not die falling."

Bellerofonte halted in surprise, but then he smiled like a demon.

"Neither did I."

Bellerofonte drove the barbed black stick into his enemy's chest, near the heart.

Bellerofonte jogged back toward his kite and then to the hatch beyond it. He considered how he would gain access, then find a place to shed his disguise. Maybe he would be so brazen as to be the one to first shout for security.

He pulled at the hatch, but found it locked. Of course.

This struck him as supremely funny, and he laughed so hard he had to sit down.

Then, wiping his eyes, he considered the mess he was in.

He had to launch from the Pupil.

Bellerofonte rose up and hurried to the green hang glider.

He saw the black hang glider, how much closer to the Pupil it was, and wondered.

He jogged over to the black kite and gave it the once over. Surprisingly, it appeared to be airworthy, and he started laughing again.

He switched helmets with his enemy. He also removed the green-labeled stick from the corpse, so only the black one remained.

He took up the black kite and hobbled toward

the Pupil.

He chuckled, wondering how long it would take the hive to find the one janitor with the hatch key. And that guy was probably blind drunk on his own homemade moonshine, it being a game day.

At last Bellerofonte was close enough so he lifted up the kite and started jogging toward the edge. He could not move very fast, but he was in a wind tunnel.

He launched into the Big Hole, into the surf roar, and worked to climb high, circling around. The roar grew louder as he was seen, and then another surprise came, the chant of "Olé."

At first he was stunned. How could they be celebrating his vengeance?

Then he realized that they took him to be black, and thus they cheered his presumed victory over that unsporting green.

Bellerofonte hoped to fly out of the eye but it took all his skill just to keep gaining altitude. He saw his only chance was to shoot back through the airway.

Soon he would enter the six hundred foot long tunnel. With the wind at his back he would lose altitude for every one of those feet. After that he would emerge from the north-facing Small Hole, in the shadow of the hive. From there he would fly over sunlit lands, riding thermals, and make his escape to the mountains.

But now each turn he made in climbing upward seemed like another victory lap. He was succeeding beyond his wildest dreams. Unseen by the TV cameras, he was close and personal to the multitudes that cheered louder and louder, and he knew he was flying into legend.

CALI-FORWARD!

2. Assignment: Agitprop

I t is autumn when The Handler meets with The Author to give guidance on the new project:

"Your weak novel *Labor Martyrs* has made a favorable impression upon the parlor pinks," she tells him, "so a sympathetic newspaper will commission from you a series of articles. For this you will travel to the interior, to the steppe lands, the Great Plains, once the Breadbasket but now the Dust Bowl. There you will write about the homeless, the freed serfs, the lumpenproletariat, as they make their way along Route 666 to California. Forward, to California! Whether you actually deal with the smelly displaced persons is up to you: what is required is stirring stories of social hardship. All of their believable blood, statistical sweat, and theoretical tears. These are your articles, for which you will be paid and awarded a

Pulitzer."

"I honestly fear that fascism is coming to America," says The Author, a man in his mid-thirties with a dark chevron mustache and pale eyes. "The American Legion is clearly the back-bone of a homegrown fascist movement. These migrants, poor white trash uprooted from their generational soil, will provide the catalyst for chaos and the rise of a charismatic fascist."

"Yes, yes," says The Handler. "Now then, it is important to have a variety of statements on the origin of the Dust Bowl—"

"It is all the fault of greedy bastards," says The Author, fervently.

"Of course, comrade, of course. The kulaks and the bankers, or the molemen with their rocket-ships and their weather-control machines. But still, there may be a time when it is better for you to tell them that the Great White Chief, who is father and mother to them, has no idea of this Farm Collectivization—it is all the subversive work of his ministers. If only he knew, he would set things right immediately . . ."

But The Author is already lost in vision, try-ing to harness it to a plan as his finger smoothes his mustache. He sees all too clearly that the Okies and the Arkies will be beaten by one group of fascists, the pool hall vigilantes, and exploited as cheap labor by another group of fascists, the aristocratic landowners. Simple agrarians, the mi-grants were being uprooted from the land of their fathers and now made pilgrimage to the Promised Land, the golden hope of California. But California is in fact the land of goose-stepping corporate agriculture, where they would be merely industrial workers in factory fields. Ultimately worked to death, and disposed of like stripped cogs.

The local police will not stop the vigilante mobs: at best they will merely stand by and observe; at worst they will join in to harass and beat the migrants.

The Okies themselves are children of nature, violent and quick to anger. They have an exaggerated politeness to signal this, and sudden murderous rage will follow if a man believes he has been disrespected. They are savages in this way, and thus even more prone to manipulation by savvy operators.

Picture the family, straight out of Lil' Abner. There is Abner, strong as an ox, dumb as a post. Then Mammy Yokum, with her knockout punch, and her hardworking ways. "Hardworking" since the "wimmenfolk" in Dogpatch do all the work in house and field, the men being useless loafers. The prime example being Pappy Yokum, so lazy he does not even bathe himself. Yes, hygiene is an important theme here, "As any fool kin plainly see!"

3. The Manager

Down there by Bakersfield, a government-run labor camp called "Dogpatch" sprang up, second of a projected many to be scattered across California. Part of the New Deal, Dogpatch shelters three hundred people, affectionately known as "campers," in tents and single room tin cabins. The tarry scent of government-issue carbolic soap rises up like the incense of civilization.

All led by The Manager, a government employee working for the FSA (Farm Security Administration, formerly Resettlement Administration). In his forties, having a hatchet face with a Chaplin mustache. Like a missionary, teaching his charges class consciousness and fundamental hygiene. Like a shepherd, protecting his flock from the predatory types lurking outside the fence. Shaping them from imbecilic individualists into the produce-picking proletariat they were meant to be, the agricultural workforce of tomorrow.

Still, even the New Deal gov't is not sold on the idea of migrant labor camps, so The Manager is fighting for his job. The main task is shifting the numbers, trying to make the forty percent of rural migrants into a majority, perhaps even an implied hundred percent.

All that fudging takes a backseat when The Author comes down. This seems like the break The Manager was hoping for, and he throws himself into helping The Author.

He gives The Author a tour of the camp. The Manager is trying to shape the tour, a little "Potemkin Village," perhaps. Takes him around to other camps: the "Hoovervilles," those squalid, verminous hobo jungles; the farm-run camps that are too much like feudalism, serfdom, or company towns. Better to have gov't do it, to ensure that there is no profit motive, and thus no way for the workers to be exploited.

Driving up the Central Valley, The Manager rants on the fascist newspapers, headed up by "His Satanic Majesty, Caesar Augustus Hearst."

The Author counters with a diatribe on fascist Hollywood, where Gary Cooper is leading the Hollywood Hussars, a squadron of movie stars who wear uniforms and practice horseback maneuvers. "That ain't no polo team," he snarls. "One of these days Gary's Goons will act against some migrant workers, breaking up a strike, and it will be just like in *Labor Martyrs,* the Cossacks against the serfs all over again."

They get along fine.

In their week of rambling up and down the state, The Manager discovers a lot about The Author. Being a manager, he is part psychologist, and through various little tics and tells, he pegs The Author as having a complex about working class men, in part due to his middle class upbringing, his household of sisters, and his failure to earn a degree despite years at Stanford. The Author exhibits a visceral repugnance for the laborer, an obsession with their genital scratching, their spitting, their sheer physicality. But at the same time he shows an almost pathetic yearning for that masculine virility: his eyes brighten when a man takes up a heavy tool in those meaty hands; he is quickened at men working on a car engine, or hearing one tell of a fistfight.

Back at the Bakersfield work camp, The Manager sets up a "Day's Wages Challenge" to encourage the campers to open up in telling their stories to The Author.

The Manager wants to rig the game, so he scouts around in the camp for the right kind of colorful characters that might impress The Author. The problem is that less than half of the Okies he has are rural folk, most of them are displaced urbanites. And the few Okie folk he has are shy and quiet. Still, The Manager vets them as best he can, but he also lines up a few hobos for their storytelling abilities. These shameless wrecks won't clam up in front of a stranger, Hell no!

Well, the first hobo starts off kind of slow, but

then gets onto the topic of prostitutes. This Cassa-
nova of the campers tells about the time he took
three in one night. Then that other time with the
one-legged gal who charged him extra.

Next!

The second hobo is mumbling around until
The Author asks him about abortions, and then he
goes on for a while about girls trying to fix their
own problems "theirselves," using such items as
knitting needles and paschal candles.

Next!

The third hobo, seeing how the others went,
spins up a cock and bull story about how he came
to California as a boy with his folks. Through one
misadventure after another, at the age of fourteen
he ended up separated from his kin. So he was
starving to death at a Finnish farmstead where the
woman had a nursing infant . . .

"You mean a woman, a girl you didn't even
know, put her milk-heavy bubs in your mouth?"

"Yessir. It's a fact."

The Hell it is, thinks The Manager. *It's a Farmer's
Daughter Story without a punch line. Wait, hold
up, it's a theme in art, in painting, at least. What's
that one called? It's religious, whatever it is. 'Milk of
Human Kindness'? No. 'Sweet Charity'? Close! Roman
Charity, that's it: Roman Charity!*

The Manager holds his breath, expecting that
The Author will see through the hobo's mask to
the college dropout within.

But instead The Author smiles and says, "We

have a winner! That'll be the ending note."

0. Okie Madonna

What a day! It was March, and Florence's migrant family had finished a beet-picking job in the Imperial Valley desert down by Mexico. They piled into their trusted Hudson and headed north to get in on the lettuce harvest at Watsonville, up near the coast by Monterey, a trip of more than 600 miles. Wouldn't you know it, at around the 400 mile mark the car broke down, and they rolled to a stop at a pea-pickers' camp filled with a few thousand people.

The pickers were having a bad day, too, since a freezing rain had ruined the crops.

Florence's husband and a couple of her boys went to town for repairs. She set up a temporary camp using the same equipment they carried for a job, and settled in for a wait, keeping her other five children close.

Originally from Oklahoma, Florence had been living in California for ten years since she left the Cherokee reservation at twenty-two. For six years she had been a migrant laborer, following the crops like cotton, beets, and lettuce, each in their turn through the seasons, but she had never seen a crowd of this great size.

She felt bad for all those pickers and their hungry little children, but she also wondered if they would get to the lettuce fields before she did. If only her Hudson were repaired!

She was apprehensive about the crowd—things could get ugly. She was watching for her husband—the sooner he came back, the better. Like a mother hen she sat, with her younger daughters beside her while she nursed a baby on her lap.

Instead The Photographer appeared, somewhat disoriented by her drive of 250 miles from the north. A woman in her forties, she walked with a limp that was due to something more than just the hulking ten-pound camera she hauled around. She snapped pictures of Florence over ten minutes, then limped away.

1. The Photographer

The Photographer was trying to keep her gov't job with the FSA.

In the balancing act between "Science" and "Art," she tended toward the "Art" side, so her field notes suffer in comparison to those of an anthropologist. In the back of her mind was the challenge to make a dog look like a cat. The tension between the common notion "the camera does not lie" and the hidden reality "the camera always lies."

The Photographer believed that "migrants" were victims of "mechanization." In her FSA photos the "mechanization" part falls out, but the victimhood goes strong.

Her "sex story" might be about how she left her artist husband for the FSA scientist whose brainchild was the migrant labor camps project. She had two sons, the scientist had three children; within a year they had divorced their spouses, married each other, taken all the kids.

Or maybe, more steamy, the difficult relations with her first stepdaughter, when The Photographer's husband was old enough to be her own father. The Photographer was 28 then, the girl was thirteen; the age gap so small that the putative mother was more like a big sister. The three of them lived in a tiny house so the girl heard their "wrastling."

In an effort to improve things between them, The Photographer took photos of the girl, including one headless full frontal nude that became the most famous. This did not improve things, nor did it end the marriage. As the years rolled by, The Photographer had first one son, then the other, and at the fourteenth year she started gov't work, meeting The Manager at camp Dogpatch.

The Photographer's dust bowl migrant pictures, which gave image to the project, are paired with a reprint of The Author's newspaper article that gave words to the project. By this point The Author has moved on to a massive novel to forward the project.

4. The Book

The journalism experiment over, The Author struggles at turning this material into a novel:

So they are pilgrims, Israelites walking across the desert to the Promised Land. Maybe they are like the pilgrims of The Canterbury Tales. *That gives a good cross-section of society, providing a couple dozen colorful characters, sprinkled with bawdy humor in graphic detail. Medieval Chaucer was a government worker writing lewd stories and social satire for his fellow government workers to enjoy. The Knight, the Doctor, the very naughty Lady of Bath. Was it the Inn Keeper who joined them? Lots of adultery and fornication, it was the "Tijuana Bibles" of the day.*

Okay, so start at a roadside diner in Oklahoma, where the waitress with a heart of gold throws in with the whole lot of them, joining the quixotic pilgrimage for Big Rock Candy Mountain. But no, the Canterbury pilgrims are just tourists; these Okies and Arkies are like Israelites who have been sold a bill of goods, trekking across the desert from one slavery to another.

Let us see, how far is this Okie Odyssey? From Oklahoma City to Bakersfield is a thousand miles, or thirteen hundred. But all by car, which really deflates the Israelite metaphor. Say it takes somewhere between ten days and two weeks. Stops along the way are gas stations, diners, and those filthy hobo jungles. Huh, more like the Canterbury pilgrims after all, which was what, three or five days? "Sumpin' like dat."

The Author goes to meet The Manager at Dog-patch Camp. It has been a couple of years since his first visit, and The Manager again tries to guide him through a Potemkin village, but immediately The Author runs into the "Doctor" and takes a shine to this shady urban migrant.

Afterwards The Author says, "With that Lenin beard, he looks half Christ and half satyr."

"That's the truth. His official job title is 'Marine Biologist,' but really he is an abortionist."

"Making him The Doctor (of abortion)?"

"I suppose. The funny thing is, one of the guys in his tent is a klansman."

"Really? Which one? Who is The Knight (of the klan)?"

"Never mind that. Thing is, the klan goes after abortion doctors."

"You don't say! I had no idea. What a potential for drama."

The Manager feeds The Author field notes from his staff writer Sanora. The Manager travels with The Author to a number of places, even down to arid Needles at the Arizona border. The first California city that the Dust Bowl migrants arrive at, Needles is the oasis before the brutal desert crossing to Bakersfield.

"Do they cross Death Valley?"

"No, but it is bad enough."

The Manager's "sex story" is like a mixture of two biographical histories for the fictional Canterbury pilgrims: the Lady of Bath's marriages and the Knight's itinerary of exotic foreign lands visited in the crusades. We start with his wife Edith, a nurse; and she was nursing a newborn, her second child, on the day that The Manager, age twenty-four, ran off with Nancy, a sixteen-year-old heiress. Is it worse if he planned it in advance, or if he acted on impulse when he encountered the girl by chance at the train station?

The bishop of San Juan married them in Puerto Rico, and then they skipped out just ahead of the private detectives hired by her family. The couple crossed the Caribbean, ran to ground in Venezuela, where they hid in a slum while he worked at an oil field. A jaunt through the Amazon jungle to shake off the flatfoots, then Alaska, followed by almost two years in Guam, where he taught school and she had a couple of babies. Then to golden California, where he sank into a dark spiral of drink and depression until he again abandoned a wife and children.

"Maybe The Knight finds out that The Doctor performs the service on Negro women."

"I don't follow, but you're always too deep for me."

"There could be an interesting coming together. Perhaps The Knight learns that The Doctor performs the service at a reduced rate for Negroes, and this stirs him so much, this nobility, that The Knight puts aside his prejudice and offers to pay The Doctor enough to make up the difference."

"A bounty, for black babies?"

"Well, he would not put it that way."

"Seems off topic, begging your pardon. Sounds like a story for Old Dixie."

"Indeed. Something for Faulkner, perhaps."

"Right, where here we are looking at the folk movement of rural whites across space and time."

The Author calls the novel one thing, then another.

The Handler names it.

The Author likes the name for its "Biblical" connotations.

The Handler inwardly laughs at this stupidity. The name comes from "The Battle Hymn of the Republic," a tune used by the victors of the American Civil War. All an allusion to the American Civil War that must come. In the next few years.

Which is to say that in the Bible the phrase comes from the Apocalypse.

The Book is published in April.

In August it is banned in Bakersfield. The farmers do not like the way they are portrayed. Most of the migrant laborers do not like the way they are portrayed as white trash, a stereotype they are already struggling against.

The Book is burned in Bakersfield. One copy. By three farmers in an alley. Hardly on the scale of the Nazi book burning rallies, which took place on college campuses; this Bakersfield incident is more like a publicity stunt.

5. The Director

Production on The Movie begins six months after the publication of The Book; a remarkably short time, perhaps a record.

The Director is trying to make a Hollywood motion picture from a mess of a novel. He streamlines The Book, sanitizes it, and uses the iconic mode established by The Photographer's "Okie Madonna." So it becomes a stirring tale of brave pioneers from "the Dust" rather than from the Old World, all on a "stagecoach" ride through "Indian Territory." Nothing about re-education camps.

The hero of The Book, a hard-drinking, fornicating, ex-con for murder, is transformed into a Young Abraham Lincoln, rail-splitter, Honest Abe. The folk are not white trash, they are displaced yeomen, honest and hardworking.

Farewell, floozies! Arrivederci, Roman Charity! Bye-bye, ball-scratching!

The Director hires The Manager as a technical advisor for The Movie, paying him a lot of money. Shortly thereafter The Manager retires from the FSA.

The Movie is released nine months after The Book's publication. The Manager, technically a bigamist, marries a nurse named Lena.

In April The Book wins a Pulitzer Prize.

6. The Troubadour

The Bard of the Dust Bowl wanders the wide land, trying to make a buck, trying to spark a communist revolution, birthing a new genre of music.

Born in Oklahoma, The Troubadour is a middle-class urbanite rather like The Author, but where The Author is repulsed by working class males, The Troubadour so embraces the rustic ideal that he makes for himself an "Okie" persona that seems increasingly comical, stereotypical. He is an avowed commie, and has a regular column in a communist newspaper for a while. He aims to put the "trouble" into "troubadour."

At the age of twenty-four he leaves his wife and three kids back in the dust to come to California. In Los Angeles he works at a radio station performing hillbilly music. Then he performs some protest songs. He meets The Author.

He moves to Manhattan. When he gets to the record company, the producer urges him to make a song about The Book. The Troubadour writes a six-minute synopsis of The Movie, and it goes onto his first commercial recording, The Record.

The wife and kids join him in Manhattan, a shaky reunion.

Then, in an adverse reaction to the tune "God Bless America" being on the radio all the time, he writes The Song:

"Oh, my loving mother, Yes I'm a Bolshy
"And I believe in the Godless Rusky
"We'll kill the Kulaks, and Kill the Bankers
"Forward to Socialism-land!
"Oh, my loving father, Yes I'm a Commie
"All property is theft to me
"We'll kill the Kulaks..."

Sure, he borrowed the tune, but ain't that always the way? The Song will become his biggest hit.

7. The Project

All in all, The Project is going strong. There are seventeen migrant work camps in California.

The Author embarks on a coastal sea voyage to discover his masculinity.

The Director wins an Oscar, his second, for The Movie.

The Handler, rendered sterile by abortion, divorces The Author upon discovering his adultery.

Then the Japanese bomb Pearl Harbor, and things go on hold for a few years.

"BUILDINGS ROMAN" BY W. DEAN

The following is a novel attempt to view an architectural history through the eyes of a hypothetical building of the day. Rather than considering a full lifespan stretching from roughly 200 BC to AD 300, this work will offer a brief sketch of the childhood period, then focus on the vigorous passage from adolescence (30 BC) to adulthood (AD 117).

Ancient Roman architecture was the offspring of Greek and Etruscan traditions. The Greek post-and-lintel construction fused with the three primary Etruscan elements (the semicircular arch, the vault, and the dome), given birth through the innovative introduction of concrete (circa 200 BC).

King Philip of Macedonia said of this Rome, "It was not yet made beautiful in either its public or private parts." Building materials were simple: ashlar work and mud brick persisted, despite the new mood of luxury that favored marble; and earthenware pediments were still common. Let us name our structural protagonist "Bill." His Republican structure is low and squat, his exterior is scruffy and somewhat brutal, and his feet are still muddy from the schoolyard. His growing pains of grade school (wars, revolts, and civil strife) mark the transition to another stage as the principal roads and aqueducts are established.

The Augustan Age (30 BC to AD 14) gives rise to the teenager. Augustus boasted that he "found Rome a city of brick and left it a city of marble," and the statement is no exaggeration. A return to peace after the transitional conflict (civil war, matriculation to middle school) drives the engines of construction. A sudden growth spurt, a state of constant erection, and an obsessive interest in the female form are all features of this period. Our building would suddenly stand in marble: a forum by day; a public bath at night.

The Julio-Claudian Age (AD 14 to 68) is a tumultuous period. The camp of the Praetorian Guard (AD 21 to 22), built by Tiberius at the instigation of back-stabbing Sejanus, was the first public building to have brick-faced concrete. Bill, our protagonist, is now a juvenile delinquent. He slouches like the Praetorian camp in a militant, menacing way, ready to spring out in violence and rage. He has lost some of his adolescent luster, probably due to the betrayal of a so-called "best friend," maybe over a "good" girl, who is to say? But Bill is toughened now; he has been bloodied.

Caligula's chief works were villas (which ringed the city) and temples (most notably those of Cybele and Isis), both devoted to the exotic and the erotic. Freewheeling Bill is getting pretty deep into the Mysteries of Woman right about now, probably in the back seat of his car with some "bad" girl from the wrong side of town. But the party is over when Claudius backs into the throne, and just as the emperor reformed the system, so does our Bill sober up from his debauchery in order to finally go to college as protection against the draft. There, however, Bill falls in with a crowd of radicals.

Contrary to popular belief, Nero was not responsible for the fire that destroyed half of the city's center (AD 64), and in fact his role in the aftermath compares favorably to that of Sir Christopher Wren (whose plans to rebuild London after the Great Fire of 1666 were ignored). Using the latest technology, Nero rebuilt the city in a stunning new image, including his public baths and his Golden House; as Martial once noted, "What worse than Nero, what better than Nero's baths?" Just as Nero has been wrongly condemned, so has innocent Bill been blamed for the fire that gutted the Federal building during a period of student protests, and he spent his time equally divided between the private debauchery of a bathhouse attendant and the public penitence of community service.

Another civil war ends with a new dynasty, that of the Flavians. Okay, now the party is really over, says Bill to himself. You are twenty years old, time to get your act together. Vespasian (AD 69 to 79) begins the Colosseum. Cut your hair, go to school, get a major with a future outside of jail. Titus (AD 79 to 81) barely has enough time to finish the Colosseum and the Triumphal Arch. What kind of major? Business? Art? Music? Domitian (AD 81 to 96) is one of the great empire builders, and his crowning achievement is the imperial residence the Palatium (AD 92). Okay, now you are twenty-one. Legal to drink and you're a teetotaler. That's fine, but you still do not have a major. Nerva (AD 96 to 97) does not have time for anything. How about architecture? And then you see it all laid out in clean lines on the draftsman's table, your own life in architecture: the muddy foundation of the schoolyard; the brick-faced adolescence; the awkward groin pains; the draft and the draftsman; the icon of the Tarot Tower burning, a beacon to your destiny; brutalism, pomo, neoclassical; the sacred and the profane, the scaffold and the profit, the mortar and the mortarboard. And it all comes spilling out in hot spurts for a History of Architecture term paper, like glowing rivets knitting together I-beams into the skeleton of myself and my calling, pins to bind flesh exterior to bone interior, hiding the engines of air conditioning respiration, sewer-line digestion, and fever fire-control from the eyes of outsiders. Man as building? Homo Erectus; Empire State Human; the riddle of the Sphinx who watches the pyramids, waiting for them to hatch.

Trajan (AD 97 to 117) definitively completes the complex of monumental piazzas, temples, and other public buildings begun by his predecessors, thus heralding the maturity of Roman architecture and the end of this *Bildungsroman.*

THE GRAY-HAIRED GIRL

I t all started when I helped this little old lady.

I was on my lunch break over at Sandwich a Go-Go and this frail granny was having trouble getting into the unisex restroom with her walker. Basically, she fell down, and nobody moved to help her. I don't think it was complete callousness—it was somehow preserving dignity all around to allow her to get up under her own steam, or something like that. Besides, who wants rejection, or worse, a lawsuit? But after that initial moment of hesitation I made like a gentleman by helping her up.

"Thanks, sugar," she said, her words slurring. "Ginny's having trouble today." She gave me a sly look. "Could you help me with my diaper?"

She meant her incontinence underwear, which she had . . . *soiled* is the word. She was not ashamed at all, in fact she was kind of coming on to me. Was she really so demented, or was she drunk as a skunk? I took her name to be a diminutive of "Virginia" that perversely sounded like a type of alcohol, fitting for a wisecracking drunken party girl.

I helped her as much as I could without compromising modesty or dignity. That is, I got her situated in the room, told her to knock when she was ready to come out, and then I beat a hasty retreat. After a long while I heard her signal, at which point I dutifully helped her as I had promised. I thought that would be the end of it.

She surprised me by sitting for a cup of coffee, during which she told me about how she was leaving her "old man," whose name was apparently "Tucker."

Hearing all this, I thought she was heartbroken and either off her meds or just drunk, which was why she was acting the way she was. Over her shoulder I saw a big obese guy come into the shop and make a beeline for our table. With his stringy long hair and loud tee shirt, he seemed the type you'd see working at a comic book shop.

"Come on, Granny," he said softly to Ginny. "Come home."

"I won't," she said, frowning at her coffee. "I found a new friend. I don't need you."

He looked at me then, his babyish face hostile for an instant. But then, apparently judging me innocent of conspiracy, his features softened, radiating embarrassment and regret as if he wanted to apologize for my being dragged into this difficult family situation. He was a 20-something like everybody else and it was touching to see him caring for his grandma, who looked like she was 70.

"We're just talking," I said, trying to extract myself, however awkwardly. I felt a strange twinge of guilt, as though I were selling her out.

"That's right," she said, rising up. It seemed like she was giving in, but then she deftly turned it to her advantage, saying, "Same time tomorrow, sugar."

She kissed me on the cheek as I tried to recover, then she shuffled out with the guy behind her.

The next day I was at the shop again. It was unusual for me to go there two days in a row, but I found myself half-watching for Ginny to come through the door. She was a colorful character, a 70-something who acted like a 20-something, and I didn't want to miss the appointment, even if she hadn't meant it seriously. Having helped her once, I felt oddly protective toward her—I didn't want to let her down, and if she didn't show up then I would still have done the right thing.

Before long I noticed the guy at the counter pointing me out to a woman. She thanked him and brought her coffee over.

"Excuse me," she said. "Did you talk to Gin-Ginny yesterday?"

"Yes," I said. She was plain, sort of old-fashioned in her dress and makeup. I wondered if she was Ginny's daughter, and it seemed plausible.

"I'm glad to meet you." Her smile of relief was pretty, and I noticed there was no wedding ring on her hand. I stumbled over the notion that she could possibly be the obese guy's mother, since she couldn't be that old. "She's come back home now and I think you saved her life. Can I sit down?"

"Sure," I said, deciding that she was Tucker's young aunt. "Please do."

"I've been so worried about her," she said as she sidled into the chair. "It's been months, but then she called out of the blue after talking to you. What did you say to her?"

"I don't know."

"Whatever it was, it worked." She took a sip of coffee. "She's in detox now, but she made me promise to keep this coffee-date with you, so you wouldn't feel stood up."

"Thank you," I said. "It wasn't really a 'date.'"

"I know, she told me," said the woman. "I guess that made you special."

"I hope she gets better soon."

"She will," she said. "She's only seventeen, and they—"

The coffee came out my nose.

"Sorry," I said, cleaning up with a napkin. "I didn't know she was so young."

"Kids these days," she said. "That crowd seems —well, my daughter took it too far, even for them."

Maybe you already know about it, but at the time I had no idea about this nameless subculture of false grannies. I had thought of Ginny as a quirky individual having a bad day, not as a representative of a group of silver vixens. I was horrified and repelled by it, since it seemed so opposite of everything.

Soon we finished our coffees and parted without exchanging phone numbers or anything. I came to regret that lack of contact info, because this meeting with her mother wasn't the end, it was more like the real beginning. Now that I could see it, the clues and cues were everywhere. And I wanted to know more, finding myself an accidental "hero." Had I really done anything to save Ginny?

At the farmers' market on Saturday I paid close attention to all the little old ladies, looking for dark roots in their hair and aging makeup on their faces, and I managed to find five fakes in two groups. They are always in groups. The drugs they take are what should be called "performance degraders." Because they appear to be old ladies, the eye skips over them quickly, the mind dismisses them, and they are marginalized into a kind of invisibility.

They exploit this invisibility. That's why they do it.

On Sunday I found two more fakes feeding pigeons in the park. I sat on another bench and pretended to read a book while watching them. After scattering the last of their stale bread, they got up and shuffled over.

I devoted myself to my book.

One of them came into my personal space to stroke my left arm.

"Mmm, so soft," she cooed about my cashmere sweater.

"Pet me, love me," I said, playing along.

They tittered at that. I grew bold.

"I have a friend, a lady like yourselves, named Ginny," I said. "Do you know her?"

"Poor dearie," said the one, now stroking my arm with sympathy.

"It's not good to speak of the dead," said the other.

"That Tucker, he's a bad one," said the stroker.

"He's got a problem," said the other. She glanced around to make sure we were alone. "And I don't mean the eating. He's a deviant."

"Myrtle!" said the first, halting mid-stroke.

"Well, it's true," said Myrtle. "He ruined her."

"We don't do that sort of thing," said the stroker, petting again.

That startled me. After all, she was stroking my arm, and based on my one encounter with Ginny I assumed that they were a promiscuous group—I had thought I was playing along. In fact they are the opposite, a female chastity society. Paradoxically, their desexualized nature allows them the freedom to pursue a kittenish hedonism, as was the case of my cashmere-stroker.

I'd thought I was secretly observing them, but they were allowing me access—they had approached me because they knew I had helped Ginny. Their granny network has eyes and ears everywhere.

I think they become fake-grannies to escape the constant sexual predation of our times and enjoy life as seniors, to find a childhood none of us had. But no armor is perfect—Tucker was the sort of deviant who wanted a fake as a lover, and it seemed as though Ginny had fallen from their graces when she became his sex slave. Ginny must have increased her degraders to dangerous levels because of his pressure on her. And being ostracized by her peers didn't help.

They are silver children, like the Eloi of *The Time Machine,* and Tucker was a Morlock.

In the following weeks I studied fakes in the field, like some kind of subcultural anthropologist. As I learned new details about their strange behavior I either laughed out loud or scratched my head. But then one day, just like the journalist who had been investigating bikers until he suddenly morphed into a Hell's Angel, I wasn't laughing any more. That was when I quit the library.

I remembered times spent talking about old movies, and saying how the glamorous adult world they show seemed to be lost to the present. Now I knew that there were no adults anymore, there are only children, 20-somethings, and senior citizens. The wave of youth-culture had been that total. If you are tired of acting younger than you really are, you have to look back fifty or sixty years to see adult-culture. You start by rejecting all the gadgets, the portable telephones and music devices, the household computer and the television set. You search the thrift stores for the old-style clothes, but you find them at vintage boutiques, where you learn the difference. You become like the Amish, in that you reject technological "progress."

The problem now is that, because your age and your clothes are so far out of sync, you stick out like a Zoot Suit at the riots. So you gain seven years in one night by graying your hair and using stage makeup to appear older. It's like Civil War re-enactment, but as a lifestyle instead of a weekend pastime.

Now you can "play 40" for decades, but only in a part of town where nobody knew you from before. You build a new persona.

You're saying, "But why do it?"

Because it felt good to be an adult, even if I was just "playing." I was like Frank Sinatra, on top of the world and in my prime, looking for my Rat Pack. I wasn't another 20-something Peter Pan anymore, I was a man, and it felt good.

Good for a while, at least. I wasn't finding my Rat Pack and it was getting as lonely as *Nighthawks at the Diner*. So I cast my net wider, visiting new parts of town. Searching.

Tonight I saw Ginny again. It took me by surprise, my first time in a new place.

"Hello," she said. "My name is Ginger and I'll be your waitress."

"Ginny!" I said, making her flinch.

I tried to pick it up on the rebound.

"You look . . ." I started, but what could I say? She's a teenager. "Good. Healthy."

"Thank you, sir," she said with a weak smile. Her face was closed now and I kicked myself for my blundering. "Are you ready to order?"

I ordered, waited, and ate, all the time trying to figure out what to do to make things better with Ginger, who had once been Ginny. I wanted to get to know her, but lurking beneath that, hidden down at the root, I suddenly realized I wanted to be her lover. Like she *owed* me that, for my saving her life, or for her changing my life. Crazy, I know, but it built on itself, making my thoughts even more scattered.

She brought the check. I took her wrist.

"Gin-ger," I said, by accident using the same sort of hesitation her mom had used. "Your mother says I saved your life. Can't we talk?"

"You?" she asked, searching my face.

"*You,*" she breathed, recognizing me. Her face opened for an instant, then clouded with confusion as she saw my condition—my grayed hair, my aged features.

I let go of her. She moved to sit down, then remembered her job and jerked back upright.

"I'm sorry," she said.

"No, I'm sorry for upsetting you," I said.

"Thank you, for before," she said.

"You're welcome," I said. "I know this is not a good time for you, can we talk later? What time do you get off?"

Even as I said it I heard it like a pick-up line, which made me ill.

"No, I can't talk later," she said. "I can't talk now."

"Not even coffee?" I said, knowing that was a mistake even before her eyes flashed.

"You're a part of the past that I have to break off with."

"But we were never—"

"I know," she said.

It felt like we were passing each other on an escalator, with Ginger going up while I was going down. No, it was worse than that. I was an adult Frank Sinatra and she was a teenage Mia Farrow. I had become a Morlock.

"Okay," I said, giving up. "All right."

"What are you even doing in this part of town?" she asked, suddenly on the verge of tears now that it was all over.

"Just one question, sweetheart," I said, getting out my wallet. "I didn't mean to save you—I mean, I didn't know anything, so I don't know what I did."

"You talked," she said.

"But what did I say?" I asked, putting the money on top of the check.

She leaned forward to take the pile of paper, her eyes brimming with tears.

"'Act your age,'" she whispered. She straightened up and said, "Thank you. I'll be right back with your change."

"Goodbye, Ginger," I said, and that's when I left.

POST-MODEM
ALCHEMY

1: Derivation. The California Gold Country had become a place of retirees and outlaws, and the Master, known by some as "Gianni the Ounce," was something of both. He practiced a curious form of alchemy such that one summer noon several elemental forces mingled in the Sierra foothills, thereby creating a magical being. In the soundless thunder came a kaleidoscopic tumble of images: his eyes, paired like the wings of a butterfly, flitting through the woods; the cabin, dark in mourning, its driveway blocked by toppled trees; his limbs being torn off; tears flowing down his face while he talked through a wall; the white column of water falling from the sky.

At first Chalmers Little was just a pair of eyes. He fluttered down from the sky and through the forest like a monarch butterfly, coming at last to the end of a new logging road. The Master called this place "Thunder Grove," and he was there with the hierophant, striking archaic postures, chanting the ceremonial language full of hums and buzzing. They disrobed and engaged in a stylized grappling. Chalmers would have laughed at the sight if he had possessed a mouth at the time—two old guys, like pink beetles, all elbows and knees, one climbing on top of the other, both humming, buzzing, shouting.

Bored, Chalmers floated away from the clearing, with its perforated cans and scattered brass casings, and into the forest. He found a shady spot and fell asleep. When he awoke he found he had a body, one that was as small as a four-year-old child and ravenously hungry. He tried eating everything: leaves, banana slugs, animal droppings, but nothing eased the gnawing pain. As fate would have it, three teenage girls found him and took him to their little bush fort.

He was the answer to their dreams, a living doll, a feral child, a forest creature. They took turns feeding him food, including their own blood and virgin milk.

After some time and countless adventures, he left the girls and the Mother Lode country to wander for several years among the coastal cities. Looking back on it later, Chalmers could not easily remember those years, but apparently he had picked up many technical skills in his brief learning stage, so that there were times when his hands knew what to do, even if it was all a mystery to Chalmers.

Then the pendulum of his life reached its farthest stretch and he drifted back. He was hitchhiking Highway 49 when the Master picked him up, and even though Chalmers was a teenager now, by arcane signs they recognized each other. So the Master took him to the cabin, put him to work as a handyman, and paid him well. Chalmers would never stay more than a week or two, expressing a tendency to drift with the season changes. Seeing this, the Master sometimes gave him odd jobs to do in out of the way places.

After completing one of these errands in the seventh year, Chalmers walked down the familiar dirt road toward the cabin. It was spring; the pine trees were green and the road was pale orange. At the gravel driveway Chalmers saw work to do: two small trees had fallen. He would cut them with the chainsaw, stack the logs in the back. Suddenly the cabin stepped out from behind a bend, golden wood with cinnamon streaks, but it was not its usual big and friendly self; it was dark, sad, and forlorn. The Master had died.

There was little to learn in the hills, because the Master had been a loner, so Chalmers walked a shortcut to Sacramento. There he met with the hierophant, who wept as he told Chalmers about the Master's final months. "He left the cabin to you," he said. "You have to pay taxes on it, every year—do you understand? You have to earn money, enough to pay the taxes. You also have to do the spring clean up every year. These two things: taxes and clean-up."

"We had some good times," said the hierophant. "We sure did. There was That Day. The sunlight cooking the ground where trees had stood. The smell of fresh cut wood, machine scent, a whisper of diesel, a trace of splattered oil, and the man smells, oh, the man smells! We fired our guns and there was lead, the smell of cordite, hot gunmetal, and the spent brass glittering at our feet. The smell and feel of bear grease, and there in the temple of raw masculinity we added the quintessence, the fifth essence, and the doorway between worlds opened for a moment."

"And then you saw the butterfly," said Chalmers.

"Butterfly?" said the hierophant, looking puzzled. "What butterfly?"

"My eyes," said Chalmers. "Coming down."

The hierophant sighed, started to say something, then stopped. He shrugged and picked up his previous thread: "It was a glorious day, a priceless moment now twenty years past. Then that night you appeared out on the deck, just a little thing, begging for food scraps with all those raccoons! What a time! But all that is gone now—he is gone."

The hierophant refused to visit the cabin, so Chalmers returned alone. He sat in the living room as evening began, when the quiet deepened into a silence that was thick and profound. Even the humming refrigerator grew silent. Then he heard a faint gurgling from below, like that of water running down the drain pipe from a shower or a flushed toilet. As Chalmers considered this in growing awe, there came a new sound, a slow but regular thump, which was unmistakably the tread of a man. But where? Outside on the deck, amplified by the drum-like surface? Down the carpeted hallway, from the Guest Bedroom, or the room that Chalmers called "the Son's Tomb," or the Library, or the bathroom? No, it seemed to be coming from above, from the cramped attic, where there was no room to stand upright.

The tread came closer and closer, until it was directly overhead. And then without a break in the rhythm the tread went past, moving away. Somewhere near the chimney there was a third sound, as if a bear had growled, or a door to a noisy room had opened and then closed.

Or as if Chalmers's stomach had growled with hunger, as it did again. He noticed that his digestive system made again the gurgling noise, while his heart beat the stately tread. His horror found a new focus: his own body had become so alien to him that he had externalized its sounds.

2: Development. In the gold country of California, the hills between Sacto and Tahoe, spring is a season of raking and burning. By law, all the leaves and needles around every structure must be gathered up and set ablaze in order to reduce the chances of wildfire in summer.

Raking and burning: he had done this with the Master for six years, and now he did it alone. Raking leaves from the upper slope down to the burn area behind the cabin. Filling the two-wheeled barrow with golden leaves from the lower slope, hauling it up the road, up the driveway, across the deck, and dumping it near the burn area.

The whole project took around eighty man-hours. When it was done Chalmers went away again, just as he always had before.

Things were always breaking down in his absence. A tree fell and smashed a section of deck railing; toilets malfunctioned; faucets dripped; the roof leaked; the drum belt on the dryer broke; a deck beam support rotted through; the fan of a bathroom heater made a grinding noise. A pipe froze and burst: his hands got the tools and did some sweat soldering. Every time he struggled to repair something, it seemed as though things were breaking down faster than he could repair them, and he thought, "Things would be better if I could live here year round." But there were no jobs in the county and he needed money to pay the taxes. Given this ratio of burden to reward, he always asked himself, "What am I doing this all for? Could I just sell the place and leave?"

In this manner the years went by.

Chalmers avoided the Son's Tomb. The Master's

son had slept in that room on his visits, and he later left many boxes of personal belongings in storage there prior to going on his travels abroad. But that was before the Master died, and there had been no sign of the son in any of the many years since. If the son were to appear one day, Chalmers would gladly show him everything about the cabin and then walk away from it forever. But he did not expect the son to appear because he had never seen the son, whose visits always seemed to happen whenever Chalmers was not around. So Chalmers suspected that the son was an elaborate hoax, a joke that would have its punchline if he became molded by the things in that room.

One summer day Chalmers went into the Son's Tomb searching for a tool he remembered seeing there once. He lingered too long, and the things there began to shape him. As he crawled out of the room, coughing and choking, he had a near-death vision in which he saw: the three girls at the Gypsy Camp feeding him; a bare foot upon the stair; a woman carrying a chest down from a height; a trunk floating on the pond.

He went outside to stand on the deck to breathe the quiet stillness, the pooling afternoon shadows. His gaze swept across the towering pine trees and stopped in the upper branches of one, where a bit of sky seemed somehow brighter blue. No, it was not sky that he saw, it was something like a star bright enough to appear before sunset. A few inches below it there was another pale blue light, smaller and less intense than the first. The branches moved with a breeze and the second light flashed green.

Chalmers reasoned that it was something reflective caught in the tree. With binoculars he failed to see more. It must be foil of some kind, a strip or ribbon of reflective, flexible material. Like a shiny helium balloon, but although he looked for the large disk of such a balloon, he could not find it. Maybe the balloon had foil ribbons.

He got the BB gun and shot a few times, aiming above the blue star, hoping to hit a hidden balloon. Nothing happened. The idea of a flying object being trapped made him vaguely uneasy. The balloon almost seemed to be alive and suffering, in which case it was better off "dead."

Chalmers went inside the cabin for a glass of water. As he drank it by the kitchen sink, he heard a sound of tiny bells on the stairs. He stepped over and looked up to see a nun of Central Asia ascending the stairs, bare feet appearing from beneath her dark robe. She disappeared at the top of the stairs. Chalmers ran up the stairs and searched the upstairs room, the bathroom, and the closet, but nobody was there.

The lights were still in the tree the next afternoon, and that made him happy. He saw the woman on the stairs a few more times before they figured out that if they held hands she could step off the stairs and into the cabin, rather than disappearing when she stepped off the first or last step.

Her name was Ai-yaruk and she said she was from Samarkand. She seemed to mean it literally —that she was walking on some haunted stairs in Uzbekistan when she suddenly ended up in Northern California. Their conversation was often jumbled, full of ambiguities—Chalmers thought her English was not very good, Ai-yaruk claimed they were talking another language. She was the most beautiful woman he had ever seen.

On her third visit, Ai-yaruk said, "I will get you new clothes."

"Why?" said Chalmers. "These are fine, and when they become worn out, there are more in the closet."

"They are dead man's clothes," she said. "And new shoes, too. Here, give me, I take shoes, pants, long shirt, get new ones."

"But—"

"You want to be the dead man, like the dead man come back to life?"

"No," said Chalmers. "I know I'm not him, and I don't want to be him."

"But you wear his clothes," she said. "Why do you avoid the storage room, huh?"

"Because those things in the Son's Tomb make me start to change."

"Yes, that's right. You are like the lizard who changes color to be invisible. If you are not willing to become the son, then you should also avoid becoming the father." She smiled. "Don't worry, I'll take care of it all for you. Sell all those clothes, sell all those things, give away what I can't sell."

"But it seems like such a waste of clothing," said Chalmers.

"The way you are doing is a waste of your life, your personality! It influences you right now. It frightens me that his suits fit you so perfectly, it scares me that his shoes fit your feet. You start to look like those pictures of him. I don't want you to be him, I want you to be you. Besides, we need the money."

"But who am I?"

"I know who you are," she said. "You are Chalmers Little."

She did all the things she said she would do. After Ai-yaruk had gone away and Chalmers was alone with his new clothes, the silence began descending like thick snow. Once again the refrigerator halted its humming and there came a strange sound, this time going: "tick-boom, tick-boom, tick-boom." He smiled, remembering the time before, and he wondered what parts of his body were making these noises. He marveled at how the sounds seemed to get louder. Through the window he saw motion, a man lurching by with a cane in the autumnal twilight.

Chalmers turned on the light and opened the sliding glass door just as the man reached it.

"Hi," said Chalmers. He saw the stranger had one leg, and only one arm. "Can I help you?"

"Yes, I think you can," said the man. "May I come in?"

"Yes, of course. Please come inside."

The man hopped in, leaned his cane against the couch, and said, "Let me take your arm."

Chalmers immediately presented his arm. The man held him at the elbow and Chambers started them toward the barstools by the butcher block.

"Pardon my asking," he said, "but who are you?"

"Why, don't you know me?" said the man, his eyes darting to the corners of the room. His hand now gripped Chalmers's shoulder. "We're practically brothers, you and I. 'In the name of the Master.'"

With that he pulled Chalmers's right arm so that it tore from his body. In terrible pain Chalmers saw black swirling mist roiling in from the edge of his vision. The floor stood up, something heavy hit his left side, and the mists swirled so tightly that there was only a peephole to see the carpet. Then this tunnel vision winked out as his leg was ripped away.

When Chalmers woke up later he began learning to get by with one arm and one leg. The stairs were out of the question. He crawled and wiggled down the hallway. Climbing up onto a bed seemed impossible, but pulling off blankets was nearly as bad. He slept on the floor.

A few days went by. Life skills were difficult and exhausting, food preparation in particular. At the end of the third day he heard scratching at the sliding glass door. He crawled over to find his stolen arm and leg wiggling around on the deck. As he saw them his heart lifted: the hand of the arm waved tiredly; the foot of the leg thumped the deck like the tail of a happy dog.

The re-membering was even more painful than the dismembering had been. When he woke up he was whole again and it was time to leave the cabin.

3: Duty. When Chalmers came back for the burn season, he was happy to see that "star" in the pine tree, winking blue and green in the late afternoon sunlight. He went inside to get a glass of water, but hearing the sound of small bells on the stairs, he turned and there was Ai-yaruk. He took her hands to help her across the threshold. They embraced, making happy little sounds.

"Hey," said Chalmers. "Come outside and see this."

Out on the deck he pointed to the "star." By turns she was surprised, curious, intrigued, and finally determined. She went back into the cabin without a word. As she mounted the stairs Chalmers called, "Where are you going?" She did not answer.

Chalmers shrugged to himself, looked back up at the "star." Ai-yaruk suddenly appeared on the roof, giving him a jolt of alarm and confusion, but then he felt awe as she kept climbing up beyond the roof, treading a stair he could not see, heading for the star in the tree. She was forty feet above the driveway, then fifty, then sixty. Chalmers ran below, hoping to catch her if she fell, but at the end of the driveway he just stopped and watched.

Then she was up there, looking so big next to the treetop, looking so small so high in the air. From his position he could no longer see the star. Ai-yaruk leaned forward, reaching both arms into the branches, and she leaned back, pulling out a wooden treasure chest. She turned and descended the invisible stairs, and Chalmers saw that the chest seemed to lack a lid. It was at least two feet long and he wondered how it could have been up there.

"Look, Chalmers, look!" she cried.

"It's—it's!" said Chalmers. "I don't know what to say!"

She was on the roof. "Come see! Come see!"

He was already running. There she was at the top of the stairs on the second floor, bright and happy. She set the chest down on its runners as Chalmers was just clearing the stairs.

Even on second glance, Chalmers saw the contents of the cradle as a doll.

Ai-yaruk continued to come and go. Chalmers stayed with the baby. He did not go anywhere, he did not do anything else, he was living there full time. The cabin, once a place of refuge, had become something like a prison. Where once time seemed to rush along, now each day dragged on and on, locked in frozen time, standing still.

Before long, vacationers at neighboring cabins saw the Little baby, and eventually the county sent a nurse to check on the infant. After that first visit it became vaguely clear that baby should be fed some factory stuff called "formula," which was fine with Chalmers because he was tired of gathering up milkweeds for her insatiable demands, even with the help of the ants who brought her bushels of grain in their tiny jaws. Nurse said that baby would gain weight and grow rapidly on formula, and she did, in a series of growth spurts. The last one was so rapid that her skin could not keep up, her skin was holding her back, and so she molted.

That was a month or two before her second summer. At first Chalmers thought there was a doll in the crib with her, but then he realized that it was a hollow thing of skin and hair—the outer layer that Baby had shed. So they called it 'Shell,' and as the months turned into years, Shell became more active.

Shell had no eyes. When her eyelids were open you could see she was hollow. So Baby used crayons and drew some eyes on her eyelids. Shell learned to keep her eyelids closed during the day.

It was during a week when Ai-yaruk was gone, as the little ones slept one late afternoon and Chalmers sat stupefied in the living room, thinking, "If only I could be still enough I could figure out what I want. If I could isolate myself from the influence of others and their demands, their expectations, their assumptions; if I could free myself from their shaping, I might be able to sense what my own goal is and then be able to work for myself toward that goal."

So right then and there he tried to be very still, to quiet himself so that he might hear himself, and then that sound came again, that series of noises that had so frightened him so long ago—the even tread, not the broken tread of the half-man. Knowing that it was the music of his own body, he listened with a fascination. The footsteps, coming closer, somewhere above his head. His heartbeat, of course; could he slow it right now? And what within him had made the door-opening sounds last time?

The footsteps stopped.

Chalmers held his breath. His heart was still beating.

A new sound, a pounding began, with muttering.

Chalmers ran upstairs, where it sounded like a person was banging on the wall from the outside.

"Hey!" he shouted in fright.

"Dogboy, is that you?" said a voice unheard for several years.

"Master!" he cried as the tears began to flow.

"What the hell's going on?" said the Master's voice. "I can't see anything but this bit of wall!"

"The wall, Master?"

"Yes, the wall! This one part, near the roofline, where I'm hitting right now. It's hovering in mid-air."

"Unpainted," said Chalmers. "That's the only part that we didn't paint—"

"Paint? You painted the Lodge? 'We'? Who told you to paint?"

"It was my idea," said Chalmers. "The weather was beating the place. And all the tin circles, it looked so trashy. So first we put on a coat of primer—"

"Who?"

"Ai-yaruk, a woman—"

"A woman! Dogboy, I warned you about them, did I not? Remember the story of the monk and his son: 'You know not which mouth you will feed.' Was it her idea? I'll bet it was, that's just the sort of thing they do."

"No, no," said Chalmers. "It was my idea. It was sometime before Baby came—"

"'Baby'?! My rage is towering at your words. I command you to tell me the whole story at once!"

Chalmers did so, telling of his development and duty. When he was done, the voice behind the wall said, "Dogboy, Dogboy—I set you three simple tasks yet you have wandered far and wide. How do they call you, that you forget everything?"

"Master, I am called Chalmers Little."

"Who gave you such a name? Where did you

find it?"

Chalmers thought back to those dark days when he came to the cabin alone. Lost, he wandered further around the pond, into unknown territory, and there he met the far neighbors, the retirees. Those cabins, so big and nice, well maintained, on good lots.

"It was Merry," said Chalmers. "Of Frank and Merry."

"Those philistines!" cried the voice. "Another witch. Play their games, if you must, but do not forget your true name. You are Jason Dee."

Whole forgotten chapters of his early life opened up for him at that name, but gaps remained.

"Master, who is the one with one arm and one leg?"

"That's Jeff Mamjay," said the voice. "Beware of him, for though he has a certain amount of cunning, a certain raw fire, he is flawed. He was the first moonboy, and you were the second, a big improvement. But the two of you combined are still not as good as my son of woman born—"

Jason noticed that his hands were trembling. As he watched in astonishment they held each other.

"Jason Dee, listen to me," said his Master's voice. "Open your mind. Remember the exercises? Open your mind now."

His hands were moving, the one writing letters on the palm of the other: NO DO NOT

"Jason Dee, clear your mind now."

HE WILL TAKE YOUR BODY

The Master's voice began chanting in the ancient language. St. Elmo's fire began sparking and glowing in the air, flickering on surfaces.

LIKE THE OTHER TOOK LIMBS

Here was the fork in the path, here was the purpose for which he was created, and now that he had arrived at this long dreamed-for moment, it looked like a cliff he was being ordered to leap from.

Though his cheeks were streaked, his eyes were now dry. He turned and went down the stairs, then went out on the deck. From the utility closet he got the ladder and the paint; he climbed onto the lower roof and finished the job, ignoring the muffled shouting that finally ceased as the last bit of bare wood was covered.

Then he cried again for what was forever lost, and he was granted a third vision: long conversations with people now dead about "new creatures of the new world," with frightful names like "green recluse," "sonsettler," and "bratskiller"; on hands and knees he climbed the invisible stairway that Ai-yaruk had walked, and reaching a landing, startled an eagle that was dozing there with wings stretched out; the third volume shifted as he lifted it down, and opening it he found the book completely hollowed out, filled not with a flask or a map but a coiled white rope, faintly purple, that resolved into a large worm that hummed a low drone and spoke oracular wisdom; stepping through the burning leaf pile and emerging from a burning leaf pile in another country; Chalmers saw Jason Dee submerged in a swamp, his face pointed skyward, his chest and arms underwater.

4: Decline. When Baby was around two years old, the county started taking her one or two days a week for something they called daycare.

When Baby was around three years old there came a day when Chalmers heard her talking at the end of nap time, so he walked into the first bedroom (once Library, now Baby's Room). Baby was sitting up, but she looked over in surprise, saying, "Where she go?"

"Who?" said Chalmers, as he moved to pick her up.

"Mermaid," she said, still looking around. "Go. Go there." Pointing at the doorway.

He picked her up. "What color was her hair?" he asked, suspecting that she was thinking of that cartoon with the redhead mermaid, a video he knew she had seen at daycare.

"Black," she said. "You come, she go. She there. Go there." Now he understood this last phrase as the command she meant. He carried her into the hall. No mermaid. "Go kitchen." No mermaid. Baby became more agitated. "Go stairs." They went upstairs. They searched through the cabin, until finally Baby said, "She gone." Such a sad little voice.

"It's okay," he said, hugging her. "Don't be sad, you'll see her again, I'm sure of it. Next time you see the mermaid, will you tell her something for me?" She nodded. "Tell her that I'm sorry about what happened the last time I met her. I was a teenager, but there is no excuse for what I did. Can you do that?" She nodded solemnly. "What will you say?"

"Charmer sorry. Very sorry."

Then county took Baby away for preschool and he only saw her once or twice a month, but by that point he had his hands full taking care of Shell. Ai-yaruk lived in Sacramento then, working at some job, driving up to the cabin for a weekend every two weeks or once a month—when she visited she insisted on sleeping in a separate bed. He asked her about this, and she said, "Incest is bad."

Chalmers felt an icy chill touch his heart but he shook it off, certain that there was a misunderstanding. A simple word mistake.

"Don't you mean 'insects'?" he said with a hopeful smile. "I know you hate—"

"No," she said. "Not bugs. I mean people. People who are related by blood."

"I still don't know—"

"I thought you were *human*," she hissed.

The sun was shining, the trees were green, and the

two men were walking on a road of pale orange dirt. Chalmers thought, "It is almost as though we were friends."

The other man was "Dmitri," also known as Jeff Mamjay, or "J. F. Mamjé." Dmitri stopped, panting with his hands on his knees. "How . . . much . . . further?" His hands did not match.

"I'm not sure," said Chalmers. "I think it is somewhere close around here." He was lying; they had passed the turn-off a few miles before.

"I can't . . . believe . . . the Master . . . would hike . . . so far."

Chalmers shrugged. "Don't forget the motorcycle."

They pressed onward. At the top of the slope there was a "T" intersection, with branches heading northwest and southeast, but Chalmers led them to the hidden footpath that turned the "T" into a cross. They followed this to the northeast, toward the mountain. The path opened into a road.

Sometime later they were on an earthen bridge over the culvert of a noisy creek. Dmitri said, "Hold up, I gotta take a leak." He picked his way down the northern side, one hand on the wall of sandbags against the bank, and emptied his bladder into the rushing water. As he was climbing back up, he said, "Hey, what's that sound?"

A continuous muffled roar, like a stationary jet. They looked up the narrow little gorge of the creek, through all the trees and shadows, and up at the top of the rise they saw a bright white spire against the blue sky, a falling cataract of water that was taller than the gorge.

They rushed toward it like hare and tortoise: Chalmers would scramble his way up the steep side, and chancing upon a new view of the waterfall, he would become spellbound until puffing Dmitri caught up. Up, over, through the bushes. The side became so steep that they feared falling.

Finally they worked their way to a little spur that offered a flat spot to stand upon. They could go no further, but they were only twenty feet from the waterfall, and truly it had no rock face, instead falling straight from the air. The waterpoint appeared out of nothing at treetop level, as if there was a hole in the sky through which poured a constant torrent of water.

"Feel that power!" Dmitri yelled over the sound. "No wonder he called this place 'Thunder Grove.'"

Chalmers smiled and turned back to studying the water. This place was not the place the Master had taken him, the clearing where the "thunder" was from gunfire, the place of his nativity. He had never seen this place before, he had never even heard of it.

The return to the cabin was all down hill. Dmitri now had a jaunty stride as he hummed *Peter and the Wolf,* while Chalmers began to puff a bit as he tried to keep up.

When they arrived at the cabin they found Ai-yaruk reclining on the lounge chair on the deck, watching the two girls playing with pebbles and sticks in the dirt. "Hi there, Yucky," said Dmitri. Ai-yaruk ignored him. "Could I bother you for a glass of water?" She got up and moved into the cabin. "Hey kids, daddy's home."

Shell looked up, puzzled, then looked at Baby. Without looking up, Baby said, "He means Chalmers."

Chalmers himself was initially irritated at Dmitri's words, but seeing the four of them for that one moment, Ai-yaruk, Dmitri, Baby, and Shell, he felt a wild hope that they could somehow be a family—that he could take one step backwards and disappear.

Dmitri laughed, sat down on the top of the steps. "You like stories, don't you? Then listen to this one, a present from me to you.

"Once there was this sorcerer named Gianni the Ounce, see? At that time all the other magicians were trying to make gold out of other things, I mean, that's all they wanted to do, but Gianni the Ounce tried his hand at other skills, like talking to the dead, conjuring spirits from the other worlds, and finally astral travel, travel to the other worlds. He wanted to see the worlds between the words, the forest inside the trees, if you can imagine that, and he became obsessed with it."

"Upset with it," said Baby to Shell.

"No, no," said Dmitri. "I mean he liked it so much he didn't want to do anything else." He turned to speak to Chalmers. "Jeez, kids! Make even a simple story a challenge. I don't know how you do it."

"True," said Ai-yaruk, who had just come out. She handed him the glass of water.

"Ah-ha. Thanks. Well then, okay—so as part of this big project he had, Gianni the Ounce needed a magical servant, like the ones that Coppélius and Geppetto had, so he made a man out of oak and he named him Jack. Now Jack was strong, and active, and able to endure all sorts of things, but because Gianni the Ounce botched some part of the magic, Jack came into this world with only one arm and one leg. Even though he was so crippled, Jack set out to do whatever jobs the old man gave him.

"Gianni the Ounce tried again to make a servant, and this time he fashioned a man out of wax. While this creature had both arms and legs, he lacked a certain inner drive, he even lacked a personality. He was as malleable as wax, and so his name was Joke. Where Jack was bright and active, Joke was dim and passive.

"Then one day old Gianni the Ounce set off on a grand expedition onto the astral plane. His spirit was gone so long that his body began to stink, really stink—"

"Stinks like poop," said Baby. "Oo, stinky!"

"Yes, that's right, and the guys Jack and Joke did not know what to do anymore. They knew they were somehow supposed to do things to help and resupply their Master on his quest, but if

Gianni the Ounce had told Joke any instructions, it had gone in one ear and out the other, and if the old man had written any instructions for Jack then they were lost in the papers. Jack went through all the papers, looking for instructions or clues, and found nothing he could act upon. He even started to figure that if there had been written instructions then Joke probably burned them up in the fireplace without having the slightest idea.

"So Jack tricked Jason—I mean, Joke—into lending him an arm and a leg. It wasn't so hard since he was wax, after all. Then Jack was nimble and quick, and he went out to find a group of alchemists. He told them something of his origins, and their eyes lit up. 'Oh,' they said. 'Gianni the *Ounce.*' See, they thought that the ounce in the Master's name was for the gold ounce, and Jack had to try real hard not to laugh since he knew that ounce was a cat name, like lynx.

"Anyway the alchemists gave Jack some help, a new arm and leg, and he found things for them, including the long lost Fountain of Wealth. He was finally on the road to success, but when he tried to share some of this wealth with Joke, that wax dummy would have nothing to do with it. He preferred to be a hermit, master-less and master of no one. But even in this 'freedom' he had no freedom, he was just a tool left behind in a workshop, a tool picked up and used by whoever happened to come around. And the workshop itself had become an open port of entry, a bridge between worlds, and Joke did not have the sense to charge a toll for the mongrels that passed through.

"And so Jack gained a kingdom and lived happily ever after, while Joke became a hermit swineherd and faded into oblivion."

"But Jeff," said Chalmers, and Dmitri's eyes bugged out as he heard that name. "You left out the son."

For an instant a ripple of rage passed over Dmitri's face, but then he smiled slyly. "No, there was no son," he said, condescendingly. "That was just another joke." But his eyes still glinted in their jovial crescents.

Baby was always gone away now, and Ai-yaruk was, too. Dmitri was gaining money and followers by leading hikes to the strange waterfall. Chalmers was wrung out, worn out, somehow used up.

One night he was awakened by the sound of a voice singing, somewhere over at the pond. He listened until it stopped, then he fell asleep. The next night he heard it again, so he walked through the dark trees under the spangled sky, down to the edge of the pond where the song abruptly ended with a splash in the middle of the water. He went back to the cabin but had difficulty falling asleep.

On the third night he carried the cradle down toward the pond. The same cradle that had first been the size of a breadbox when they brought Baby home in it had grown along with her until they moved her into the crib. It now weighed around fifty pounds. He set it down so he could rest, and he wondered why he did not put it in the car and drive to the pond, but then he remembered that the car was the son's car and had not run in several years.

Sweating and straining, he set the cradle down on the first dock and then went back to the cabin. He picked up Shell, glanced around for anything else, grabbed her favorite little blanket that had once been Baby's. Back at the dock he put Shell and blanket into the cradle, heaved the cradle into the water, and pushed it toward the deep end.

He watched it until it disappeared, somewhere near the middle of the pond.

He never heard the singing again.

5: Dissolution. Now that he was free, Chalmers found that he could not move, he could not get away from the cabin. It had been so effortless before, when he would simply walk up the dirt road, take the middle fork, and find himself at Sacramento or the coast. But now the middle fork was gone, and even when Chalmers pushed his way through the overgrowth, he only came out on the other side.

He tried walking without the shortcut but it was several miles to town and his attempts at hitchhiking failed—the drivers did not seem to see him at all. The trek to Growlersberg, a place founded in the gold rush and still looking for a reason to exist, took most of a day and all of his energy. He slept in a park and hiked back to the cabin the next day.

In growing desperation he tried starting the car, and when that failed he opened the hood and let his hands work at fixing the engine. After a few frustrating days of this he gave up. It seemed that the pendulum of his life was nearly stopped.

Chalmers began to slip into fugue states in which his mind would wander far and wide. When he came out of these fugue states Chalmers would find himself covered with dust and cobwebs. On the last time he heard the voices of two women talking, the one saying, "Whew! The interior needs some work, too." To which the other replied, "Clear out the furniture and make one pass with the Carpet Doctor, that would take care of most of it."

As he came to his senses he saw the two young women: one a brunette wearing a business suit, and the other a blonde wearing dungarees. The brunette continued speaking: "We can have it for back taxes. Replace the deck, paint the outside, and we can sell it for a good profit."

"But this room is so dark," said the blonde. "We have to bring some light in. A new window on that wall?"

"It would face the dirt bank and the next cabin beyond that."

"So then a skylight, in front of the fireplace," said the blonde.

Chalmers found his voice. "The Master envisioned a light well, centered over the kitchen table." The women slowly turned toward him. "Like the one upstairs. I've seen a sketch, in fact it is in the table. Let me show you." He walked around them to open one of the drawers, where he fished through the papers. "Perhaps he placed it further back from the fireplace so that the heat of a fire would not leave the room so quickly."

The blonde looked at him without blinking. "That's true, the heat would go right out. Instead of a light well, we could use a solar tube."

"Here's the drawing," said Chalmers, pulling it from the drawer and setting it on the table.

The brunette said, "Excuse me, but who are you?" She blinked and stepped back. "My name's Babette, I'm a realtor, and this is Michelle, she is a con—"

"No, no," said Chalmers, holding up his hand. "I know who you are—you are Baby and you are Shell." The women glanced at each other, then back at him. "Oh," said Chalmers. "You don't believe me, you can't remember, you think I'm just a crazy old kook." He turned to the blonde and said, "Shell, *open your eyes.*" Michelle's beautiful green eyes rolled up like window blinds, revealing her to be as empty as a suit of armor.

Chalmers turned to Babette and said, "There now, do you see?"

"Yes," said Babette, softly.

"You've come to take the place and I'm all for it," said Chalmers. "Sell it to a nice couple with a few little kids, won't you?"

"Yes," said Babette.

"Keep it painted, please. I mean, don't strip it and leave it that way."

"We know."

"So how can I help, besides getting out of your way?" said Chalmers.

There was a pause, and then Michelle said, "Termite inspection." Her voice was now as hollow as her head.

Babette said, "Didn't you—for the Master—crawl under the cabin once?"

"More than once," said Chalmers. "Sure. Many times. Killed the termites, did some repairs. You want me to do that for you?"

"Yes, please," said Babette.

"Well all right, let's go," he said. They trooped out onto the deck and along the side to the utility closet. Chalmers opened the door, then lifted the trapdoor and looked down at the dank, moldy dirt. In he went, wriggling and crawling, examining the walls, the pipes, and the beams. After about an hour he worked his way back to the trapdoor and called until they came.

"No termites," he reported. "The rest looks okay. Anything else?"

"Please stay down there until we call you," said Babette.

"Okay, sure," said Chalmers as she closed the trapdoor over his face. "Glad to be of help," he called as they closed the door to the closet.

"Unquiet spirits," said Michelle.

"Was he ever really born?" said Babette. "Was he ever really alive?"

"A fickle step-sister, a treacherous half-brother . . . I'd weep if I had eyes."

"I was surprised he was so nice in the end."

"He was a charmer, may he rest in peace."

In short order all the repairs and modifications were done. The patched and rotting deck was torn out, replaced with a new one. The carpet was cleaned, the exterior was given a fresh coat of paint, a solar tube was put into the ceiling by the fireplace and another one over the kitchen table, brightening the place with natural light. The water line was upgraded, a propane gas system was installed. Chalmers felt renewed and re-invigorated with each improvement, and when it was over he felt better than he had ever felt in his life.

Then the family moved in and he felt even better. There was a father and a mother like he always wanted, and two pretty little girls like the ones he had been so burdened with for such a short eternity so long ago, but these two were no burden at all. They all lived and breathed and ate and slept and dreamed inside of him. The gurgle of water in the pipes was the sound of his digestion, the curtains stirred with his breath, the creaking of the walls was the cracking of his joints.

At long last the pendulum had stilled and he was at peace. He was Cabin Little.

PUBLISHING HISTORY

"Miracle of Asteroid Camp 88" first appeared online at *Bastion*, June 2014.

"Genre Purge 3" first appeared online at *Perihelion*, November 2016.

"My Four Foundling Fathers" first appeared in *Wicked Words Quarterly*, September 2014.

"Post-Modem Alchemy" first appeared in *The Society of Misfit Stories Presents: Volume 2*, 2018.

BOOKS BY THIS AUTHOR

Tarendra

"Tarendra" is a pocket epic; a star-spanning Slower Than Light voyage of alien discovery and adventure in three parts, beginning with the story "Lightspeed Messenger" and moving on from there in bold new directions.

The Jizmatic Trilogy +

"The Jizmatic Trilogy +" (plus) is an annotated edition of "The Jizmatic Trilogy," a collection of three short stories: "Under the Moons of Jizma," "The Gods of Jizma," and "Secret Master of Jizma." A Martian mashup of "John Carter" and "Naked

Lunch."

Old Flames Burn Manvi

Twelve tales of action and intrigue, including:

*A space-suited adventure in "Mad Dogs of Mercury," regarding mercs on the innermost planet when a simple job goes bad.

*A literary who-done-it with "Hardboiled Proust," tracing trouble at a living history park.

*An alt-history through the lens of "Hitler's Hollywood," examining the alt-cinema that led to Nazi triumph.

And more!

Doomsday And Other Tours

A collection of nine stories, including:

*"The Ragnarockenroll Overture" which gives the

strange history of a mutated Asia.

*"Doomsday Tours" that has a zeppelin full of tourists visiting historical sad spots across a Europe that is in the process of buckling after the withdrawal of American forces.

*"It's a Long Road to the Sky Train" being about a woman who goes on a big trip across a strange landscape.

These stories amount to 37,000 words of content, which is the size of a long novella, or just short of a novel (at 40,000 words).

Fallout Stories

A celebration for "Fallout" with nine post-apocalyptic stories, including:

*"Fallout 1979" deals with a team of survivors going into the fallout plume in Iowa.

*"Scout Team from the Arc" is a "recontact" story regarding people leaving their underground shelter for the first time in a generation.

*"The Brave Little Trash-bot at the End of the World" is an odd one.